Chapter 1: The First Pulse

She felt the bass thrum through her chest, the lights above her dancing in an almost orgasmic rhythm. The haze blurred everything—everything except him. In that moment, she was utterly captivated. Each pulse of light caught his face just right, carving his features in fleeting flashes. The impassioned focus in his expression made her knees weaken. He stood behind the DJ decks on a podium above her, and she knew instantly she needed to know him.

Scarlett had been hitting the raves on this circuit for over a year and had never seen him before. Terry or Rob were usually the lads running the decks here—reliable only in their talent for shutting down and vanishing at the first sign of trouble. Suddenly, he looked up and locked eyes with her, snapping her out of her trance. Heat rushed to her cheeks as she realised she'd been staring—frozen and intent—for the last five minutes, the sole rigid figure in a sea of writhing bodies. He smiled at her—shy, almost hesitant—and she returned it with an awkward wave. Wanting to be literally anywhere else, she turned toward the makeshift bar.

It was basically two oil drums and a warped plank of wood, crates of random bottles stacked behind it. Three middle-aged men were manning the setup. As she approached, she noticed some of the bottles still had their security locks attached. Well, it wouldn't be an illegal rave without stolen booze, she thought.

The bar area was swarming with ravers shouting their requests over the thumping music. Scarlett squeezed herself into the mass until her waist hit the plank. She was shocked it didn't collapse under the force that slammed her forward, pushed by the bodies behind her. She scanned the crates until she spotted Jack Daniel's and raised her hand as though flagging down a taxi. Middle-aged man number three noticed her first, his eyes sliding over her with a sly grin. Ew, she thought. "Yes, me darlin'?" he drawled, accent thick with London cockney. "One JD, please!" she shouted back. "Bottle or glass?" Sod it, she decided. "How much for the bottle?" His grin twisted, turning predatory. "My kind of girl," he said, reaching into a crate and pulling out a large bottle—conveniently one without a security lock. "For you, gorgeous? Call it a tenner." She dug out the cash and handed it over. He slid the bottle across the plank and winked. Scarlett grabbed it and pushed her way back through the crowd, determined to find somewhere to sit in this cavernous old warehouse. She hated being here alone and wanted a corner where she was least likely to be bothered.

She eventually found an old wiring spool and two wooden crates arranged like makeshift tables and chairs, abandoned plastic cups and someone's discarded jacket littering the setup. Plonking herself onto the least disgusting crate, her eyes drifted straight back to the DJ. God, he's gorgeous, she thought, taking a swig from the bottle and shuddering at the bitter burn. From what she could see, he had dark hair—short at the sides and longer on top—flattened beneath a giant pair of headphones. His light-coloured T-shirt (white, maybe?) clung to his muscular chest and shoulders exactly the way you'd want it to. His face was all sharp lines and perfect cheekbones, softened by a faint shadow of stubble. He twisted the knobs on the deck in time with the music, his hips moving in a rhythmic thrust with the beat.

God, I wish Jade was here, she thought. The words pulsed in her skull almost as loudly as the bass leaking through the warehouse walls. Jade had bailed on her at the absolute last second—texting soz babe x just as Scarlett was already weaving through the industrial estate. Normally she wouldn't dream of going into a rave alone, but it was always the same crowd every week, all summoned by a cryptic Facebook post only loyal regulars knew how to decode. She'd figured she could just latch onto a few familiar faces—the kind she knew by sight but not by name. So far? Nothing. Everything felt… different tonight. Wrong in a way she couldn't explain. They'd been using this warehouse for nearly two months—every Friday, doors opening at midnight sharp—but the atmosphere was off. The lighting seemed harsher. The air thicker. The shadows deeper.

The whole decoding system had been passed down like folklore: one person teaches you the cipher, you pass it on to someone else. Scarlett and Jade had learned theirs from Jade's weird uncle Gary—sixty-five, perpetually wired, and somehow still going harder than people half his age. Jade swore she'd never seen him work a day in her life, yet he always had cash, always had a nice car, despite living in a council flat in the rough end of the city. When Scarlett joked he was probably a drug dealer, Jade just shrugged and said, "Well, the Molly for my 18th birthday makes sense now." That night had been legendary. The two of them smashed, dancing through every club in the city.

Now it felt like another lifetime. They were thirty now—proper jobs, actual responsibilities. After Scarlett got dumped two years ago (by text, of course—the worst), the two of them had fallen back into partying, then into raves, then into illegal raves because they were cheaper and way more thrilling. They'd bolted from police at least three times—once through a loading bay, twice across a field when the rave was hosted on a farm. No one wore heels to these things. Scarlett stuck religiously to her battered black Converse.

She lifted the Jack Daniel's to her lips again, grimacing as it burned down her throat. The music shifted mid-swig. The smooth, pulsing rhythm she'd been soaking in cut abruptly into a choppy, basic beat. She looked up. The DJ she'd been admiring earlier was gone—vanished like they all eventually did. In his place stood a lad who looked about twelve, awkwardly bobbing his head while playing what she affectionately called TikTok classics. Brilliant. Even the eye candy had clocked off. God, I'm getting old, she thought, and took another drink to drown the feeling.

A tap landed on her shoulder. Light. Quick. She turned—and froze. He was standing right in front of her. Him. The DJ. The one who'd smiled at her from the decks. Up close, he looked even better: warm brown eyes, shy grin, hair a little messy from his headphones. He held a bottle of Budweiser in one hand and tugged at the hem of his T-shirt with the other like he wasn't entirely sure what to do with himself. For a second, Scarlett forgot how to breathe.

Chapter 2: AJ

He mumbled something, but it was swallowed instantly by the music. 'WHAAAT?' she shouted, tapping her ear to signal she couldn't hear a thing. Oh my god, oh my god, she thought. He leaned closer, smiling in embarrassment. 'HI— I'M AJ!' he bellowed, laughing as he said it. She couldn't help but beam back at him. 'I'M SCARLETT!'

Now that he was right in front of her, she took him in properly. He was tall—easily six-two—with broad shoulders, strong thighs, and the hint of a dad bod that somehow made him even hotter. Up close, under the flashing lights, she saw his hair was brown and his eyes… God. The deepest brown she'd ever seen. She felt like if she stared too long, she'd fall straight in. Then she realised he was checking her out too. His gaze lingered—definitely on her boobs—before snapping back up to her eyes. Too dark to be certain, but she could've sworn he was blushing. 'WANNA GO SOMEWHERE QUIET?' she yelled, throwing her shot into the universe. My god, he is stunning.

He nodded eagerly and threaded his fingers through hers before weaving them both through the mass of writhing bodies. They almost smacked straight into someone—Gary. He was bouncing erratically, two glow sticks wedged between each of his fingers and one hanging from his mouth. Sweat glistened on his forehead, and his pupils were tiny pinholes. He dropped the glow sticks the moment he recognised her and pulled her into a sweaty hug. AJ hovered awkwardly beside them, still clutching her hand like he wasn't sure if he was allowed to let go.

'FRIEND OF JADE!' Gary gurned, releasing her only to grip her shoulders. 'WANNA BUY SOME KET?' And there it was. Suspicion confirmed. 'NO THANKS, UNCLE GARY!' she shouted back. 'I HAVE MOLLY AND WEED TOO?' 'I'M GOOD, THANK YOU!' she yelled, laughing. Christ, the world's oldest raver and drug dealer. Gary turned to AJ. 'WHAT ABOUT YOU?' 'I'M GOOD, MATE!' AJ said quickly. Still laughing, Scarlett squeezed AJ's hand. He took the cue and led her on, navigating toward a small door beside the DJ podium. He knocked—loudly. Turned back to her and smiled. Nothing. He knocked again, harder. Still nothing. She saw him mouth, *for fuck's sake*, before shouting, 'OUTSIDE?' She nodded, and he guided her through the exit into the crisp night air.

It was pitch black except for one lonely streetlamp across from the warehouse. Most of the buildings around here were long abandoned, with only a handful of small businesses still clinging to the estate. The canal stretched out in front of them, invisible in the dark but impossible to hear over the thumping music inside. 'You're not going to murder me, are you?' she asked, half-joking. His horrified expression made her laugh. Then he realised she was joking and smirked. 'I could ask the same of you.' He nudged her playfully. 'So your Uncle Barry sells weed?' 'Gary,' she corrected, rolling her eyes. 'And apparently so. He's my mate's uncle. I told her he was probably a drug dealer.'

AJ laughed, then looked toward the canal. 'I'm freezing. Wanna walk and talk?' He nodded toward the steps. 'Sure.'

They wandered along the canal path, talking as though they'd known each other for years. She learned that "AJ" actually stood for Arthur James. He was only DJing tonight because the usual DJ, Terry, had been arrested last week and AJ had been brought in as a temporary fill-in. He stressed that he usually only handled weddings and parties, definitely not this scene. By day, AJ was a tree surgeon. By night, a part-time wedding DJ. He was thirty-four, almost thirty-five, and a massive gaming and tech nerd—just like her. He was the second oldest of six brothers and had lived on the outskirts of the city most of his life before moving into the county.

She told him she'd recently turned thirty, worked as an associate solicitor specialising in family law, but had just completed the Bar course. "Cross-qualifying" was the plan—moving from solicitor to barrister over the next year or so, with the long-term dream of becoming a judge in the criminal courts one day. He'd listened with genuine interest, which was rare. She explained she'd grown up in the county her whole life but spent plenty of time in the city—her friend Jade lived there, and her firm's office was in an ancient Tudor building in the middle of the city centre.

They walked all the way to the footbridge, sharing swigs from her bottle of JD. By the time they looped back toward the warehouse, she could feel the warmth of the alcohol spreading into her ears on the otherwise freezing November night. Her words were getting more slurred, her giggles more frequent—and AJ was matching her drink for drink.

They stopped on the canal path in front of the warehouse, neither wanting their conversation to end. A lull settled between them, a comfortable silence. They smiled at each other. Then— 'Fuck it,' AJ said, and before she could react, he grabbed her and kissed her. Hard. Deep. His tongue slid into her mouth as she gasped in surprise, then melted into him. Her hands ran up his muscular arms, over his shoulders, finally hooking around his neck. He lifted her by the thighs, pressing her back against the cold brick of the warehouse. The wall thumped with the beat pulsing inside as they devoured each other, hidden in the shadows. Their hands roamed, eager and searching. Christ, she thought, are we really about to fuck in a warehouse car park?

Suddenly, the sound of pounding footsteps tore through the moment. Not from the door, but from the junction. A sharp shout cut through the shadows. "POLICE! STAY WHERE YOU ARE!"

Chapter 3: The Eject

AJ lowered her gently, hands lingering at her waist a second too long. His pupils were blown wide, breath warm against her cheek—God, that kiss had shaken her. And him. Definitely him. A sharp shout cut through the shadows. "POLICE! STAY WHERE YOU ARE!"

AJ's entire body shifted. Not panic—never that. Just a sudden, controlled focus that made Scarlett's skin prickle. He pressed a finger to his lips and angled them deeper into the darkness, using the thick shadows of the building's corner to conceal them. More boots thundered past the warehouse than she'd ever heard in her life. Screams echoed inside as the music cut off, replaced with chaos. The warehouse doors burst open, followed by stampeding footsteps. Someone was fleeing. Lots of someones.

Scarlett's stomach dropped. Shit shit shit. She'd been part of raids before. She'd never been inside one. If she got caught here—bar course or not—she'd be absolutely, undeniably screwed. AJ didn't hesitate. He grabbed her hand, fingers threading with hers like it was instinct, and pulled her tight to the wall. The bricks scraped her clothes as he guided her along, his movements precise, almost practiced. The sirens multiplied, echoing off the industrial estate like the whole city had descended.

He stopped at the corner and leaned out just enough to assess. She could feel his pulse in the hand holding hers. Strong. Steady. Not like a man scared. Like a man thinking. "Back way is flooded with uniforms," he murmured, barely audible over the distant shouts. "We have to go over the wall. The wall." She nodded. Hell, she'd sprout wings if he asked right now. "You'll be fucked if they catch you." His voice dropped lower. Rough. Protective. Something about the way he said it made her toes curl inside her boots.

He pulled her around the corner and practically dragged her across the open stretch. More ravers were already lined up against the wall, queuing like terrified refugees waiting for a border crossing. Others sprinted toward the gates, police giving lazy chase—they weren't the targets. Not tonight. Gary would be, she realised, heart lurching. Oh god… poor Uncle Gary. "Now," AJ said, positioning himself. Not a question. A command. It should've annoyed her. It didn't. She stepped into his hands and he lifted her like she weighed nothing. She hauled herself onto the top and straddled the wall, offering her hand. He shook his head faintly and leapt—catching the top with effortless strength before pulling himself up in one fluid motion. Jesus. He made it look like a movie stunt.

"Let me drop down first," he said, voice softening as he swung over. "I'll catch you." He lowered himself, hanging by his fingertips before dropping silently onto the pavement. Other ravers hit the ground behind him with far less grace—some stumbling, some scrambling away. "Scarlett—now! The pigs are going to clock this lot and come running."

She tried to copy him. She really did. But her foot slipped and she fell directly onto him, knocking them both into a heap on the pavement. Oh my fucking god Scarlett, you absolute idiot. Her brain screamed at her. AJ burst into laughter beneath her, warm and stunned. "Jesus—you okay?" Mortified, she scrambled off him, but he caught her hand and pulled her up beside him. That's when they heard it. "OI! YOU LOT—STOP!"

Ten officers barrelled toward the cluster of escapees. AJ didn't let go of her hand. "Run," he said, and she didn't need telling twice. They sprinted down the street, breath burning, feet slamming against tarmac. Scarlett could hear the pounding footsteps behind them, then fading as she and AJ ducked into an unlit alley. He didn't hesitate—just tugged her deeper, weaving through the narrow jitty lined with terraced houses.

When they finally burst onto a brightly lit main road, both of them sucked in the cold November air like it was holy. "They're not behind us anymore," AJ said, taking a second to check the empty road. "But we need to keep moving. Anyone looking at us right now will know exactly where we came from." He chose the direction—left—toward the glowing sign of the 24-hour Tesco. She let him lead. Her mind refused to stop replaying that kiss…the way he'd grabbed her like he'd been waiting his whole life for it.

When they reached the car park, AJ's expression softened, the adrenaline still shimmering in his eyes. "I'm going to have the best 'how I met your mother' story to tell our kids someday," he said, like it was the most natural thing in the world. Scarlett laughed, heart doing a stupid flip. "Why—planning on marrying one of the police officers?" His face flickered—something strained, almost guilty—before a smile was forced in place.

He opened his mouth to answer, but his phone buzzed sharply. He pulled it out, glanced at the caller, and instantly silenced it. Scarlett caught the name before he pocketed it: Deedee. A woman's name. Calling at nearly 6am. A cold, irrational twist settled in her stomach. Of course he has someone. A man like that? Obviously he does. She followed him into Tesco a few steps behind, studying him. Black jeans, fitted white shirt (too well-fitted), Adidas trainers, a frankly illegal arse, and— No wedding ring.

The café was open but empty, fluorescent lights humming above them. They slid into a booth. "Fancy breakfast?" she asked. "My treat." He gave her that grin again—the one that made something warm unfold inside her. "Mate, that'd be perfect. Full English. Not exactly how I pictured my night ending." She melted a bit at the way he looked at her—intensity masked as humour. "But it's my treat," he added, tapping her wrist lightly. "I owe you after one of the best nights I've ever had."

She flushed. He went to order. The kid behind the till gave him a number and AJ stepped aside to text—furiously, thumb flying, jaw tight. Definitely not a girlfriend-texting kind of vibe. When he finally slid back into the booth, he looked furious. "What's up?" Scarlett asked. "Nothing." "Oh come on," she said, nudging him. "We're basically blood-bound after that escape." He huffed, playing along. "My DJ equipment's been seized. Probably won't get it back." A lie. She didn't know it. But she felt a tug in her gut—like something didn't match. Still, he smiled at her again. And god help her, that smile made her forget every red flag she should've been paying attention to.

Chapter 4: Lingering Sparks

They finished their breakfasts slowly, the café quiet except for the hum of lights and distant tills. Scarlett kept sneaking glances at AJ, noting the subtle way his fingers drummed on the table and the way his eyes softened when they met hers. As she pulled out her phone to book an Uber, AJ leaned slightly closer. "I should probably have your number before you vanish into the night," he said with a half-smile. Scarlett felt her stomach flip. "Right," she whispered, holding out her phone. He handed her his, and their fingers brushed as she typed her number in. When she returned the phone, their hands lingered together a second too long. Sparks jolted through her. Once the ride was booked, she slipped her phone back into her pocket.

They walked toward the automatic doors at the main entrance, fingers brushing again as they passed through. The crisp November air hit her face, and she shivered. He mirrored her movement, stepping just a little closer. "Text me when you get home," she said, voice lighter than she intended. "I will," he replied quietly, thumb brushing hers. Scarlett's heart hammered.

The Uber pulled up, headlights cutting through the morning gloom. She turned to him. "Goodbye, AJ." Before she could overthink it, he leaned in. Their lips met in a kiss that was soft, electric, and lingering. Scarlett's knees nearly gave way. When they finally broke apart, she leaned back in the car, still tingling from the touch. AJ watched her slide inside, his fingers brushing the air where hers had been. He gave a small wave, and she couldn't help but grin.

He's impossible, she thought, gripping her phone and settling in for the ride home. She tapped out a quick text:

Scarlett: Made it in the car safe. Thanks for… everything.

A moment later, her phone buzzed.

AJ: Good. Sleep well, Scarlett. Can't wait to see you again.

She smiled, her cheeks still warm from the kiss. The ride began, the car moving through the quiet streets, but her mind was still stuck on him

Chapter 5: The Kyle Problem

Opening the front door, Scarlett was immediately relieved at the warmth inside. The adrenaline from last night had completely drained her during the taxi ride, leaving her shivering for the past twenty minutes as the driver insisted on keeping the window down "so she wouldn't get sick," despite her protests. He had assumed, after seeing her tight jeans and sparkly top, that she was drunk. Jonesy, her ginger cat, padded toward her, trilling a greeting. Scarlett bent down, fussing him between the ears. "Don't worry, I'll feed you in a second," she murmured, smiling at his soft purrs.

Making her way into the kitchen, the emptiness of her house struck her. AJ's presence from last night—his energy, his laughter, the danger, the heat—still lingered, leaving the rooms feeling impossibly bare. After feeding Jonesy and hanging her jacket on the banister, Scarlett felt the weight of the day press down. She trudged upstairs, stripped out of her clothes, and crawled into bed, letting the sheets swallow her. Her mind swirled with images of AJ, the raid, and the adrenaline-soaked chaos of the rave. Exhaustion finally caught up with her. She closed her eyes, letting herself drift, the sound of her cat settling in nearby lulling her into a much-needed sleep.

Scarlett woke slowly, sunlight slanting through the blinds, the quiet of her house almost alien after last night's chaos. Jonesy padded along the bed, weaving between her legs, his soft trilling a comforting soundtrack. She glanced at her phone: multiple missed calls, texts from Jade, and… Kyle. Her stomach twisted. She answered on the third ring.

"Scar! Hey, are you there?" His voice, way too chipper for someone who had caused her five years of stress, made her jaw tighten.

"Seriously, Kyle? It's Saturday. I'm hungover. What do you want?"

There was a pause. Then, "I've been doing some self-reflection. Therapy. Working on myself."

Scarlett pinched the bridge of her nose. "Uh-huh. And?"

"I… I really think we should try again. I mean, I've changed. I'm not the same guy. I'm ready for… us."

Her laugh was short and bitter. "You mean the guy who spent five years sitting on his butt playing video games while I cooked, cleaned, and basically ran the household?"

"Well… I worked, okay, kinda. But I was busy," he mumbled.

"Busy cheating?" she snapped. "Busy sleeping with Devon while stealing half my furniture and ghosting me for months? Yeah, you were really busy."

He hesitated. "I... that was—"

"Save it," she cut him off. "I'm not interested. Not now, not ever."

She hung up and pressed her face into the pillow, screaming softly. Her phone buzzed again. Unknown Caller. Her pulse jumped. It was AJ.

"Scarlett?" His voice, low and rough from exhaustion, made her breath catch. "You awake?"

"Yes," she whispered, her lips curving despite the lingering hangover. "I... survived the sleep, barely."

"Good," he said. "Listen, I need to come over."

She hesitated only a heartbeat. "Okay. Now?"

"Yes. Send me your address."

She tapped it out, fingers trembling. Within minutes, the sound of a car horn outside made her heart hammer. She hurried to throw on something comfortable, smoothing her hair and glancing nervously at Jonesy, who disappeared under the bed with a hiss.

Chapter 5: The Kyle Problem

Opening the front door, Scarlett was immediately relieved at the warmth inside. The adrenaline from last night had completely drained her during the taxi ride, leaving her shivering for the past twenty minutes as the driver insisted on keeping the window down "so she wouldn't get sick," despite her protests. He had assumed, after seeing her tight jeans and sparkly top, that she was drunk. Jonesy, her ginger cat, padded toward her, trilling a greeting. Scarlett bent down, fussing him between the ears. "Don't worry, I'll feed you in a second," she murmured, smiling at his soft purrs.

Making her way into the kitchen, the emptiness of her house struck her. AJ's presence from last night—his energy, his laughter, the danger, the heat—still lingered, leaving the rooms feeling impossibly bare. After feeding Jonesy and hanging her jacket on the banister, Scarlett felt the weight of the day press down. She trudged upstairs, stripped out of her clothes, and crawled into bed, letting the sheets swallow her. Her mind swirled with images of AJ, the raid, and the adrenaline-soaked chaos of the rave. Exhaustion finally caught up with her. She closed her eyes, letting herself drift, the sound of her cat settling in nearby lulling her into a much-needed sleep.

Scarlett woke slowly, sunlight slanting through the blinds, the quiet of her house almost alien after last night's chaos. Jonesy padded along the bed, weaving between her legs, his soft trilling a comforting soundtrack. She glanced at her phone: multiple missed calls, texts from Jade, and… Kyle. Her stomach twisted. She answered on the third ring.

"Scar! Hey, are you there?" His voice, way too chipper for someone who had caused her five years of stress, made her jaw tighten.

"Seriously, Kyle? It's Saturday. I'm hungover. What do you want?"

There was a pause. Then, "I've been doing some self-reflection. Therapy. Working on myself."

Scarlett pinched the bridge of her nose. "Uh-huh. And?"

"I... I really think we should try again. I mean, I've changed. I'm not the same guy. I'm ready for... us."

Her laugh was short and bitter. "You mean the guy who spent five years sitting on his butt playing video games while I cooked, cleaned, and basically ran the household?"

"Well... I worked, okay, kinda. But I was busy," he mumbled.

"Busy cheating?" she snapped. "Busy sleeping with Devon while stealing half my furniture and ghosting me for months? Yeah, you were really busy."

He hesitated. "I... that was—"

"Save it," she cut him off. "I'm not interested. Not now, not ever."

She hung up and pressed her face into the pillow, screaming softly. Her phone buzzed again. Unknown Caller. Her pulse jumped. It was AJ.

"Scarlett?" His voice, low and rough from exhaustion, made her breath catch. "You awake?"

"Yes," she whispered, her lips curving despite the lingering hangover. "I… survived the sleep, barely."

"Good," he said. "Listen, I need to come over."

She hesitated only a heartbeat. "Okay. Now?"

"Yes. Send me your address."

She tapped it out, fingers trembling. Within minutes, the sound of a car horn outside made her heart hammer. She hurried to throw on something comfortable, smoothing her hair and glancing nervously at Jonesy, who disappeared under the bed with a hiss.

Chapter 6: Kitchen Chaos

The moment AJ stepped into her kitchen, Scarlett felt that same pulse she'd felt on the warehouse dancefloor—the instant, jarring recognition, as if she'd known him forever. The air between them crackled, and without a word, he closed the distance. Their lips collided, urgent and desperate, clothes brushing, hands roaming. AJ's body pressed against hers, heat radiating through every inch of skin. Scarlett gasped as he tilted her back against the counter, lips trailing fire along her jaw and neck. She clutched at him, fingers digging into the firmness of his shoulders, feeling every taut muscle beneath her touch. The world narrowed to them: lips, hands, gasps, and shivers. Every caress was electric, every kiss a small explosion. Scarlett arched into him, lost in the sensation, in the urgency that had been simmering since their first glance at the DJ deck and the dancefloor.

Then—

The front door rattled violently, and a furious voice yelled: "Scarlett! I know you're in there!"

Her heart jumped. "Kyle!" she screamed, voice cracking. "Get out! NOW!"

But he didn't listen. Kyle barreled into the kitchen, face red, fists clenched. Scarlett tried to twist away, but he lunged at her, swiping with a hand meant to hit her. AJ's eyes snapped open, a low, dangerous growl building in his chest. Scarlett yelled again, trying to shove him back. "GET OUT!" Kyle, in his fury, knocked over a mug and sent a jar of utensils clattering to the floor. He tried to lunge at her again, slapping wildly. Scarlett flinched—and AJ moved. With a fluid, controlled motion, AJ caught Kyle's wrist mid-swing and twisted, sending him stumbling backward. Kyle flailed like a trapped insect, crashing into the counter and sending a stack of plates skittering to the floor.

Scarlett bit her lip to keep from laughing, heart still hammering, cheeks flushed from desire and panic.
"You're not destroying anything else," AJ said, voice low, calm, and deadly. One firm shove and Kyle tripped over his own feet, flailing like a child. AJ guided him gently but firmly toward the door.
"Scarlett! You can't—" Kyle sputtered, half-laughing, half-panicked.
AJ rolled his eyes. "You're hopeless. Out."
With one final stumble, Kyle tumbled into the hallway and out the front door, muttering curses.
Scarlett let out a shaky laugh, relief flooding her as she sank back against the counter. AJ leaned in close, brushing her hair from her face, eyes softening in a way that made her heart skip again. He didn't wait long. Their lips met once more, urgent and fierce. Scarlett arched against him, hands tangling in his hair, pulling him closer. AJ's hands roamed her back, sides,

and legs, every touch sending sparks through her nerves. Their bodies moved in a rhythm that was effortless, instinctive, and fiery.

He scooped her up and settled her fully onto the kitchen counter, the surface cool beneath her. Their clothes came off in a desperate, tangled rush, landing softly on the checkered floor tiles. His eyes drank her in—the visible tremble, the bruises, the vulnerability—before settling on her eyes, confirming their mutual need. AJ moved over her, his chest brushing her breasts, the rough stubble on his jaw scraping her sensitive skin as he trailed fire down her collarbone. His touch was firm, possessive, urging her hips to meet his. Scarlett gasped, running her hands over the taut muscles of his shoulders and back, needing the solid reality of his body beneath her frantic hands. The rhythm was fast, consuming, driven by the chaos and the relief of being safe from Kyle. She cried out, grabbing his hair, pulling him deeper, demanding more of the sensation that drowned out the fear. The tension that had coiled inside her for twenty-four hours snapped, releasing in a dizzying, shivering wave. AJ collapsed onto her, breathing hard, his full weight grounding her against the counter. "God," he whispered against her neck, the single word conveying relief and possession. When the frenzy of heat and desire finally ebbed, they sank into each other, foreheads touching, bodies still pressed together. Scarlett poured two mugs of tea, steam rising around them like a soft, intimate curtain. "How do you take it?" she asked, passing him a mug, voice soft but playful. "Builders. Two sugars," he said, grinning with that half-boyish, half-dangerous charm that made her stomach flutter.

She shook her head, pouring herself one with a generous splash of milk. "And me? Loads of milk, of course."

He peered at her over the rim of his mug. "Wait… did you scare it with the teabag?"

Scarlett laughed, almost spilling her tea. "Maybe I did. Don't judge—it's how I like it!"

AJ chuckled, leaning back against the counter, eyes soft and amused as he sipped. Scarlett rested her head lightly on his shoulder, fingers laced with his, savoring the warmth of the kitchen, the shared haze of satisfaction, and the electric pull between them that hadn't dimmed since the warehouse. *Maybe this… maybe him…* she thought, closing her eyes, lips curling into a smile. *This is the kind of chaos I could get used to.*

Chapter 7: The Unseen Phone Call

The TV flickered softly across the living room, casting gentle shadows over Scarlett and AJ as they lounged on the sofa. They'd spent hours half-watching Netflix, half-laughing, teasing, and stealing glances at each other. Scarlett felt every brush of his fingers against hers, every sigh, every murmur as if the air between them had become electric.

Eventually, AJ shifted closer, voice low and hesitant. "Think I should go soon?" he murmured, glancing at the clock, dark eyes flicking to her. Scarlett raised a brow, a sly smile tugging at her lips. "Or... maybe you want to stay over?" He hesitated, a faint trace of guilt crossing his features. "I really should—" "But baby, it's cold outside," Scarlett teased, her voice playful, referencing the Christmas song. AJ's lips twitched into a reluctant grin.

That was all it took. They moved to her bedroom, hands exploring gently, lips claiming each other with a tenderness Scarlett hadn't expected. This time, the intimacy was slow, deliberate, and entirely different from the frantic relief of the kitchen counter. AJ worked patiently, his mouth trailing down her body, his hands moving with worshipful reverence over her skin. He made sure she felt seen, adored, and completely safe. Scarlett responded by tangling her fingers in his hair, pulling him closer, murmuring his name. His weight was a solid, comforting presence over her, his movements a steady rhythm that spoke of deep, quiet connection rather than sudden need. Every touch was an exploration, deepening the strange, immediate trust she felt for this handsome stranger. This was slow and exploratory, like a honeymoon night for two people who had somehow known each other forever. AJ's exhaustion from the night before was present—dark circles under his eyes—but it only deepened the intensity of the connection between them. Fingers laced, lips brushing, murmurs of each other's names spilling into the quiet room. Scarlett felt warmth in her chest she'd never known—desire mingled with safety, thrill intertwined with trust. They moved together slowly, savoring each touch, each sigh, each whispered word, until the release was a long, shuddering wave of shared peace.

Afterwards, tangled in the sheets, hearts still racing, bodies pressed together, Scarlett rested her head on AJ's chest, listening to the steady beat of his heart. They drifted off to sleep wrapped in each other, the world outside fading away.

Sunlight filtered softly through the blinds, painting stripes across the bedroom. Scarlett stirred first, eyes opening to the warm glow. Her fingers lazily traced the outline of his chest as she lay awake, enjoying the quiet warmth between them. The serenity of the morning was broken when AJ's phone buzzed sharply on the bedside table. He glanced at it, tensed, and quietly slipped into the bathroom, trying to keep his voice low. Scarlett's curiosity piqued, a flicker of unease creeping in, and she listened carefully to the muffled conversation.

"...Yep, I'm on my way now," he murmured, tone clipped and efficient. "Shouldn't take long. Copy that."

A few brief, quiet exchanges followed. The way he spoke—casual, yet precise, almost like he was covering something—made her stomach twist with suspicion. It sounded like a conversation with a friend, maybe, but the secrecy in his tone made her uneasy. She exhaled slowly, a knot forming in her chest. Why did that sound so... off?

A few moments later, AJ emerged from the bathroom, brushing a strand of hair from his forehead. He bent down, capturing her in a passionate kiss that lingered, warm and urgent. Pulling back slightly, his dark eyes locked on hers. "I'm so sorry, there's an emergency callout at work. Huge tree down, apparently. I will definitely be back... can I call you later?"

"Of course," she whispered, heart fluttering, as he grabbed his jacket and stepped toward the door. The small terrace suddenly felt impossibly quiet without him, the house somehow emptier than it had ever seemed before. He paused at the door, one last glance over his shoulder, and offered a small, reassuring smile before disappearing into the morning light.

Scarlett picked up her phone, heart still racing from the night and the unease left behind by AJ's call. She rang Jade immediately.

"Jade! You won't believe this," she blurted, pacing her kitchen. "AJ—he's… he's amazing, but… there's something weird. You know I told you he's a tree surgeon? Well, he just took a super-secret call in the bathroom, all 'Copy that,' and then said he had to leave right away for an 'emergency tree down.'"

Jade's voice was quick and excited. "Wait, wait, wait. Netflix? Bedroom? Ohhh, I'm dying for details!"

Scarlett groaned, half laughing, half frustrated. "Yes, Netflix, yes, bedroom… yes, it was… incredible. But the call—he sounded so secretive, almost like a cop or something! And then he left for this sudden, urgent tree removal. It made me feel uneasy. I don't know what to think."

Jade's laughter was melodic over the phone. "Scar, he's clearly got secrets, but girl… you've got to be careful! But also, he's your soulmate, isn't he?"

Scarlett exhaled, holding her phone tight. "I… I think he might be. But it's moving so fast, Jade. Less than twenty-four hours, and I can't… I've never felt like this before."

"Scarlett, listen to me. Sometimes you just know. Don't overthink it. Let it happen."

She nodded, even though Jade couldn't see her. "Okay… okay. I'll try."

Chapter 8: Anticipation and Warnings

The week crawled by in a delicious mix of anticipation and stolen moments. Scarlett and AJ had texted constantly, their conversations a lifeline between work, appointments, and responsibilities.

"I didn't realize tree surgeons were so busy," she teased one morning, reading a message from him mid-coffee. "Twelve-hour days? How do you even survive that?"

"Lots of caffeine and swearing at trees," he replied with a grimacing emoji. Scarlett laughed aloud, nearly spilling her tea.

They FaceTimed most evenings, letting the hours of the day slip away as they stared into each other's eyes, laughing, teasing, sharing stories and confessions. Their connection felt effortless, yet electric, as though they'd always known each other, even though it had only been a few days. Wednesday night had been another long, raunchy evening. AJ had stayed over again, pressing close in the dim light of her small terrace, kissing her with a hunger that made

Scarlett's knees weak. By morning, they'd stumbled out into the cold November air, blinking at the daylight, both exhausted but reluctant to part. Their laughter had filled the quiet house, and Scarlett had felt the dangerous pull of attachment she hadn't anticipated—soulmate sparks mingling with the thrill of secrecy.

The rest of the week had been a balancing act: early mornings at her law firm, AJ's physically grueling tree-surgery jobs, text exchanges during breaks, and FaceTime calls late into the night. Every message, every glance, every shared laugh only deepened the simmering tension between them.

Then came Thursday afternoon, when Scarlett opened a message from AJ that made her pulse spike:

You really don't need to go this weekend. It might be… busy.

She frowned, reading it again. AJ was cautious, worried even—but Scarlett had promised Jade she'd go. Jade had canceled last time and was desperate to attend.

I know you'll want to come. Just… be careful, the message continued.

Scarlett's chest tightened, her excitement mingled with concern. She typed back quickly:

Don't worry about me. Jade's going, and I promised her. Besides… I want to surprise you.

A single emoji followed: a winking face. AJ didn't reply immediately. When he did, it was just three words:

See you there.

The weekend approached like a storm of adrenaline. Scarlett packed carefully: warm clothes layered under casual rave gear, glowsticks, and a bottle of water. She thought of AJ—her tree surgeon / part-time DJ—smiling at her, brushing past her on the dancefloor, and the thought of seeing him close enough to brush against, to share fleeting touches, made her pulse race. Tonight, she thought, I'm going to find him… and nothing's stopping me.

Chapter 9: The Forest Chaos

The week had slipped by in a haze of stolen moments. Scarlett and AJ had spoken every day—texts during breaks, quick voice notes, late-night FaceTimes where he looked exhausted but still smiled the moment her face appeared. She never realised tree surgeons were run off their feet with twelve-hour days, yet AJ still carved out time for her. On Wednesday, he'd stayed over again, and they'd had another slow, intimate night before both dragging themselves into work the next morning. By Saturday, the anticipation had built to something almost electric.

"Come on," Jade urged as they locked the car in the muddy lay-by. "The sooner we get in there, the sooner I can get hammered."

Scarlett laughed, following her along the narrow woodland trail. Fairy lights hung from branches, guiding ravers toward the clearing where the music thudded through the ground like a second heartbeat. The woods opened suddenly, revealing the rave in full swing—lights flashing across trees, bodies moving in the smoky air, and the makeshift bar already doing brisk business. And there, up on the rig, was AJ. He was mid-set, headphones around his neck, one hand on the mixer, utterly in his element. Scarlett's stomach flipped. She lifted her arm and waved. He saw her instantly—an infectious grin lit up the whole clearing. But he couldn't leave. Not yet.

"Right," Jade declared, dragging Scarlett toward the bar. "If Lover Boy's busy, we're drinking."

The hour passed in a blur of cheap vodka, sticky mixers, and laughing fits that left Scarlett doubled over. By the time AJ's set faded and the second DJ took over, she was well past tipsy—she was absolutely hammered.

He found her easily. "Scarlett," he said, appearing through the crowd, breathless from the set but wearing that grin that always melted her. She practically launched herself at him, arms around his shoulders.

"You finished," she slurred, beaming.

He chuckled, brushing a thumb along her cheek. "Come on. Let's get some air."

They slipped away, hand in hand, weaving through the trees until the rave sounds softened into a distant pulse. The woods were darker here, quieter, mist curling at their feet. A small clearing opened ahead, moonlight catching on the leaves. AJ backed her gently against the trunk of a sturdy oak, his hands braced either side of her head. Scarlett giggled, breath warm and sweet with alcohol, tugging him closer by his jacket. The kiss was instant—deep, messy, hungry. Nothing like their Wednesday night softness. This was heat and urgency and relief after a week of wanting.

AJ's body pressed against hers, the rough bark at her back, his hands gripping her waist. Scarlett moaned into his mouth, fingers threading into his hair, pulling him hard against her. He lifted her against the tree, their bodies pressed tight, their clothes tearing as they tried to get closer. Their intimacy here was raw, primal, and driven by the reckless abandon of the night. His lips and teeth claimed her throat, her shoulder, and she arched into him, seeking the pressure that would drown out the distant bass and the fear. The rough bark of the oak scraped her skin, a minor pain swallowed by the overwhelming, consuming heat between them. She gasped his name, pulling at the fabric of his jeans, desperate for connection. They moved against the tree, quick and fierce, a necessary confirmation of life and desire in the wild chaos of the woods.

When they finally sagged against each other, trembling and laughing quietly, AJ rested his forehead against hers, brushing his thumb over her swollen lower lip.

"God, Scarlett," he whispered.

She giggled, still clinging to him, cheeks flushed and eyes half-lidded. "Missed you."

"Yeah," he breathed. "Me too."

Hand in hand, they started back toward the rave. They'd barely reached the tree line when it happened. A sharp, violent crack tore through the clearing. People near the bar stumbled back as a huge branch splintered off an old pine, smashing to the ground with a thud that shook the earth. Screams. Shouts. Lights whipping around to see what had fallen. AJ instantly shifted—alert, scanning, posture sharp in a way Scarlett had never seen before. He curled his arm protectively around her waist as the crowd rippled with confusion and adrenaline.

"It's okay," he murmured, though tension coiled through his voice. "Just stay close."

Scarlett leaned into him, heart hammering—not from fear, but from the intensity of him, of the night, of everything between them. The weekend had only just begun, and already, it was spiralling into something unforgettable.

Chapter 10: The Organised Enemy

Chaos rippled across the clearing. People backed away from the fallen pine branch, phones out, lights flashing across bark and debris. A couple of lads were filming it like it was the highlight of their night; others were shouting about how it "nearly took Dave's head off." The music didn't stop, but the mood shifted—buzzing, uneasy, crackling with that strange energy raves get when something just… feels off. Scarlett clutched AJ's arm without thinking.

"Bloody hell," Jade muttered, appearing beside them breathless, cheeks flushed from dancing. "I thought someone had exploded a speaker."

Scarlett laughed weakly. "Nearly took out the bar."

AJ didn't laugh. He wasn't panicked, but he wasn't relaxed either—somewhere in between. His eyes swept the crowd, scanning faces, movements, the tree line. Not dramatic, not obvious… just focused.

Hyper-focused. Scarlett nudged him gently. "You okay? You look like you're doing maths in your head."

He blinked, then forced a small smile. "Just making sure no one's hurt. Big branch like that… could've been ugly." His tone was calm but distant, and Scarlett felt a tiny, irrational twist in her stomach. He always seemed so solid, so sure—but there was something today that hovered around him, like a storm cloud trying to decide whether to break.

Before she could ask more, a shout rose near the bar. "Oi! Someone's nicked the lockbox!" A collective groan rolled through the crowd. The organiser—massive beard, high-vis jacket, always stressed—was stomping around like a bull. "Whoever took it better bring it back before I drag you out by your bloody ankles!"

Jade snorted. "Here we go. Every rave. Every. Single. One."

But AJ stiffened beside Scarlett again. Not dramatically. Just enough for her to feel it.

"Is that… bad?" Scarlett asked softly.

"Probably some idiot trying to impress someone," Jade shrugged. "Or they're off their nut and think the lockbox contains, like, Narnia."

AJ didn't comment. His attention was fixed on something—or someone—across the clearing. Scarlett followed his line of sight but saw nothing except clusters of ravers and torch beams.

"You sure you're okay?" she asked again.

He turned to her, the tension fading from his face as he cupped her cheek with surprising tenderness. "Yeah. Just… want to keep you safe."

Her chest tightened. She leaned into his touch before Jade crashed the moment with: "Shots?"

Scarlett and AJ both groaned. Jade rolled her eyes. "Fine. Boring couple. I'll go alone."

As Jade disappeared (already making friends with a group of girls in glitter wings), AJ slid his arms loosely around Scarlett's waist from behind. She relaxed into him, the heavy thud of the bass vibrating through their bodies.

"You're hammered," he murmured against her hair.

"Mmm," she hummed. "You love it."

He chuckled quietly. "I do, actually."

They stayed like that for a moment—wrapped up in each other while the rave swirled around them, lights flickering through the trees, people dancing, laughing, drinking, drama unfolding near the fallen tree. But even wrapped in his arms, Scarlett felt it—the slight edge to him. Like he was listening for something. Bracing for something. Trying not to let her feel it.

"Do you… need to go?" she asked carefully.

He hesitated. Barely. But she felt it. Then he kissed her shoulder, lingering. "No. I'm here with you."

Warmth flooded her chest, mingling with vodka and desire and confusion she didn't have the capacity to unpack. "Good," she whispered. "Because if you disappear again, I'll… I dunno… fall over."

That made him laugh, proper and warm. "You're not going anywhere," he said, giving her a squeeze.

But the moment they returned to the crowd, the weird tension in the air thickened. People were muttering, pushing, searching. More torches lit up the woods. A couple of organisers were arguing loudly, gesturing toward the path. Something was definitely going on. Scarlett frowned. "Do you think we should leave soon?"

AJ's jaw worked for a second before he answered. "Not yet. Just stay close to me, alright?"

She nodded, though worry twisted low in her stomach. The night had started perfect—electric, fun, everything she'd wanted after a long week. And the sex… god. The tree. The way AJ had looked at her like he'd burst if he didn't touch her. But now— Now something in the woods was changing. And Scarlett didn't know why.

'Lets get some air' AJ said sternly, his jaw tense.

Chapter 11: Reckless Love

The trees swallowed the last beats of the rave, leaving only a low thrum that vibrated through Scarlett's chest. She leaned into AJ, wobbling slightly. "You know," she slurred, "this whole 'get some air' thing… could be code for 'let's do it again in the clearing.' Just sayin'."

AJ rolled his eyes, but there was a twitch at the corner of his mouth that made her heart skip. "You're ridiculous," he muttered, scanning the shadows.

"Ridiculous? Moi?" Scarlett laughed, hiccuping. She tugged at his sleeve, spinning slightly in the mist. "I'm the picture of class and elegance. Totally sane."

He tightened his grip on her hand, keeping her steady. "Mhm," he said dryly. "Sane as a firecracker in a blender."

And speaking of firecrackers... Gary appeared, as if conjured from thin air. He was dancing—or flailing—through the edge of the mist, arms twisting like he was trying to conduct some invisible orchestra. His mouth moved, laughing, yelling, cackling at nothing and everyone all at once. Scarlett stopped mid-step. "What... what is he doing?" she asked, voice high-pitched with giggles.

AJ's jaw tightened. "Gary being Gary."

"Gary being... lunatic Gary!" Scarlett corrected, pointing. "I mean, he's like... unhinged, but... adorable? In a terrifying circus-man sort of way." She hiccupped and laughed so hard she almost fell into AJ.

AJ's eyes flicked to a darkened corner of the clearing. There—a small figure slipped a black bag to another, shadows swallowing the exchange. His grip on Scarlett stiffened. "Stay close," he said low, and she felt the shift in his tone, that quiet, rigid tension that told her something was off.

"Something serious?" she asked, still tipsy but sensing his alertness.

AJ didn't answer. His eyes moved like radar across the clearing, trained on every twitch of movement. Scarlett leaned against him, trying to sober up enough to make sense of it. "You're so… vigilant. I like that."

"You like danger," he muttered. "I like keeping you from it."

Scarlett tilted her head, drunk grin spreading. "Oh, AJ. You say that like it's all serious business. I could make danger… more fun." She nuzzled his shoulder. "Round two?"

AJ groaned but didn't push her away. The way he watched her—the way he moved—told her he was holding back. Holding back from letting the chaos around them catch them off guard.

Behind them, Gary erupted into an impromptu one-man show. He threw his hands skyward, then collapsed into a dramatic bow, then jumped up again, spinning in circles like a man possessed. Scarlett laughed so hard she almost cried. "We should film him. Or… sell tickets. Definitely a circus act." AJ's hand slid down to steady her waist. "Stay focused," he muttered, though there was humor in his voice now. "Something's not right."

Scarlett giggled and leaned closer, breath warm against his neck. "You're paranoid. I like it. Makes you look… rugged. Mysterious. Dangerous in a good way." AJ didn't answer. He was scanning, always scanning. But Scarlett didn't mind—her head spun, her heart raced, and despite the haze of alcohol, she felt alive. She felt wanted. Safe-ish. Thrilled. Gary's manic energy echoed behind them as they edged further into the mist, and Scarlett caught a glimpse of the small black bag again. Something about it made her stomach twist. She didn't know what it was. But she knew AJ knew. And that was... both terrifying and exciting.

Scarlett hiccuped, laughed, and whispered, "AJ... if this air thing doesn't work... we could... you know..." He groaned again. But this time, there was a spark in his eye, dangerous and amused. Scarlett grinned. Chaos, lust, and danger—perfectly mixed.

Scarlett stumbled a little, clutching AJ's sleeve. "You know... I could be dangerous," she slurred, giggling. "You've only known me a week, and look at me—practically a walking disaster."

AJ caught her, holding her steady. His eyes softened, but there was that serious edge again, the edge that made her heart twist. "You're not just dangerous, Scarlett. You're... reckless. Since Kyle... I've seen you do things that could get you hurt. Things that could cost you everything."

Her laughter faltered. She blinked at him, tipsy and suddenly vulnerable. "Oh… wow. That's… deep, Mister DJ."

"I mean it," he said, voice low, intense. "And I can't just… stand by." He swallowed. "I don't know why this happened so fast. Why… I feel this. But I… I love you, Scarlett. I can't stop it."

Her grin wavered. "You… love me?"

"Yes." He cleared his throat, embarrassed. "I… I love your brain, the way you think, the way you see the world… your laugh, your stubborn streak… your fire. And yes… your body, too." His cheeks burned, but he pressed on. "I can't explain it. I just… need you safe. Always."

Scarlett blinked, speechless, letting his words sink in. She leaned into him, half-drunk, half-overwhelmed. "Okay… okay," she whispered. "Just… don't let go."

"I won't," he murmured, his arms tightening around her. But even as she melted into him, her tipsy bravado returned.

"But... if we're staying out here... maybe danger can be fun," she teased, nuzzling his neck.

AJ's jaw tightened. "You have no idea what's coming tonight," he muttered, eyes flicking to the shadowed corners. The small black bag from before shifted again, the exchange repeating in his mind. "We need to be careful."

Scarlett's chest tightened—not with fear, exactly, but with that familiar thrill. She trusted him. She needed him. And for the first time in a long while... she didn't want to be anywhere else. The mist swirled around them, Gary's manic energy still echoing behind them, and somewhere in the shadows, the night was waiting. Dangerous, unpredictable... and far from over.

Chapter 12: Tethered to the Threat

The mist clung to their skin as they edged further into the trees, the low thrum of the distant bass fading into a ghostly echo. Scarlett's arm looped around AJ's waist, swaying slightly with the uneven ground. "Honestly," she slurred, leaning her head against his shoulder, "you're way too serious for a DJ. You should be spinning tracks, not… scanning the shadows like a moody forest elf."

AJ's lips twitched, half-smile, half-grimace. "Somebody's got to keep you from falling face-first into the mud."

"Or getting… abducted by fairies," she giggled, hiccuping. "I like you better than fairies, you know. Way cuter. And taller."

He shook his head, amusement flickering in his eyes. "You're impossible." His hand tightened slightly on hers, grounding her. "Stay close. Something feels off tonight."

Scarlett blinked up at him, squinting through the haze of alcohol. "Off? Like… spooky off? Or… sexy off?"

AJ exhaled a sharp laugh, though it carried an edge of seriousness. "Spooky off. Definitely not sexy. Well… maybe a little scary sexy, but mostly… stay with me."

"Always with you," she murmured, snuggling against him despite the tipsiness making her wobble. Her chest fluttered in a way that wasn't just the alcohol. There was something raw and urgent in the way he held her—protective, tethered, like he didn't want to let go. They passed the edge of the clearing again, and Scarlett caught a shadow moving near the trees, something small being exchanged—a flash of black, a slip of movement. She glanced at AJ, lips parting. "Is that…?"

"Stay close," he murmured again, scanning. His eyes flicked from shape to shape, hand ready on her waist to steady her. "I don't know what exactly, but… just trust me."

She tilted her head, eyes softening. "You're ridiculous. Overprotective, moody, handsome... all rolled into one mysterious DJ package." He gave a short laugh, the corners of his eyes crinkling.

"Ridiculous, yes. But tonight, I'm serious. Keep near me, alright?"

Scarlett pressed herself to him, the warmth of his body cutting through the cool mist. "I'm with you. Always with you." And even as she laughed again, hiccuping and teasing him about his elf-like seriousness, a twist of unease settled in her stomach. Something in the air... tonight wasn't like the other raves. Something big was about to happen—and she didn't want to be anywhere else than right here, clinging to him.

Scarlett stumbled slightly over a tree root, and AJ's hand shot out, steadying her. "See?" he muttered, eyes flicking toward the shadows. "You need me upright."

"I need you," she whispered, leaning closer, breath warm against his neck. "And maybe… I need another round of… round two?"

He groaned, exasperated but not pushing her away. "Not right now. Focus. Something's about to go down."

Scarlett pouted, half-laughing, half-serious. "You're no fun. I was just trying to make the danger… more fun."

"You make everything fun," AJ said quietly, voice tight now. His gaze scanned the clearing again, sharp, assessing, every muscle coiled. "But… some things aren't for fun. Tonight might be one of those."

Her laughter faltered. "Tonight?" The playful edge slipped from her voice. She pressed herself against him, suddenly aware of the undercurrent of tension threading through his normally teasing tone. "AJ… I… I want to stay with you. I… I don't care about anything else."

His jaw worked, a flicker of something—fear, frustration, need—crossing his face. "Good. Then stay close. No wandering off, no distractions. I mean it."

Scarlett tilted her head, swaying slightly on the uneven ground. "You sound… weirdly serious for someone whose 'real job' is DJing. Are you always like this when you're protecting people?"

"Only when it matters," he said, voice low. "And right now… it matters."

She smiled softly, tipsy warmth making her bold. "You're ridiculous. But I… I trust you." Her chest tightened—not with fear, not yet—but with that familiar pull toward him, the need to cling, to stay tethered.

Then, a sudden movement in the corner of the clearing caught her eye—a flash of black slipping between trees. Scarlett's heartbeat jumped. "AJ… did you see that?"

He didn't answer immediately, only shifted slightly, wrapping an arm around her to pull her closer. "Yeah. Stay quiet," he whispered. "Something big is happening. I don't know all the details yet—but I'll make sure we're okay."

Scarlett's stomach twisted, equal parts thrill and dread. "Okay… with you."

And then, from deeper in the mist, a sound—metal clinking, a low growl of voices, laughter that didn't reach the eyes of the shadows—made her shiver. AJ's hand found hers again, squeezing firmly. "Stick with me," he murmured, voice tight. "I won't let anything happen to you."

She hiccuped, leaning against him anyway, trying to laugh through the sudden tension. "You're… ridiculously heroic," she slurred. "And ridiculously. And… hot. But mostly heroic."

He let out a short, tight laugh that didn't quite reach the humor in his eyes. "Focus, Scarlett. Just… stick with me."

And as the shadows lengthened, twisted by the flickering glow of distant lights, Scarlett felt it deep in her chest—tonight was going to be dangerous, messy, and utterly consuming. But she didn't care. She had AJ. And for now, that was enough.

Chapter 13: In the Trap

"I'm serious," AJ muttered, jaw tight, scanning the shadows. "Tonight… trouble's coming. And you stick with me. Don't wander."

Scarlett laughed softly, leaning her forehead against his shoulder, swaying slightly. "You make everything sound so… dramatic. I like it."

A faint metallic clink echoed from the trees, followed by low, hushed voices Scarlett couldn't quite make out. Her stomach twisted—thrill and fear mingling in a heady cocktail. "AJ… what is that?"

He didn't answer immediately, only narrowed his eyes. "I don't know yet," he admitted, voice tight. "But I've got a bad feeling. Something's happening, and it's… big."

Scarlett tilted her head, hiccupping. "You always say that… but this time, I think you mean it. You're… ridiculous. Overprotective… and ridiculous."

AJ's hand slid to steady her waist. "I'm serious. Stick with me. Don't… do anything reckless."

"I don't do reckless," she whispered, half-laughing, half-serious. "Well… maybe sometimes. But only if you're there."

He caught her gaze, and for a brief moment, his usually sharp eyes softened. "Good," he said quietly. "Because I… I can't let anything happen to you."

Her chest tightened at the weight of his words. *He's serious. He actually means it.* She pressed closer, tipsy warmth tangled with the sudden, dangerous tension of the clearing.

A figure slipped through the shadows, clutching a black bag. AJ's eyes narrowed. "Stay down," he hissed, pulling her behind a thick trunk.

Scarlett's pulse raced. "What… what's happening?"

"Shh," he whispered. "I don't know exactly. But something's about to go very wrong. And I don't want you in the middle of it."

Her fingers clutched his arm. "I'm not going anywhere. Not without you."

A sudden flare of light from the edge of the clearing illuminated faces Scarlett didn't recognize—masked, hurried, tense. A harsh bark of laughter made her flinch. AJ's body tensed, every muscle ready.

"Stay calm," he murmured, brushing her hair from her face. "Stick close."

Scarlett nodded, barely breathing. *This isn't just a rave… this is something else.* Yet, tangled with fear and excitement, her body responded—heart hammering, adrenaline surging, drawn irresistibly to him.

AJ's eyes met hers, steady and unyielding. "Whatever happens," he said quietly, almost to himself, "we get through it together."

Scarlett swallowed hard, tipsy grin flickering. "Together… always?"

He gave her the faintest nod. "Always."

Then, from the mist, a shout rang out—a sharp, angry bark that cut through the haze. Shadows lunged, moving faster, closer, and Scarlett's stomach lurched. The night had shifted. Danger was here. And AJ… AJ was ready.

Chapter 14: Lethal Force

The mist swirled thick between the trees, curling around Scarlett's ankles as she stumbled slightly. AJ's hand shot out instantly, gripping hers. "Careful," he muttered, eyes scanning the shadows like they were alive.

"I'm careful… mostly," she slurred, leaning closer, cheek brushing against his arm. "Mostly careful with you."

AJ didn't answer, only tensed, and Scarlett felt a shiver run down her spine. There was a sharpness in the air now, something that wasn't just the damp chill.

A rustle. A shadow darting across the clearing. Scarlett froze. Before she could react, a figure lunged at her. Reflex screamed louder than fear—she swung. Her fist connected with a solid jaw, and the attacker staggered back, cursing. Scarlett's heart pounded, her adrenaline drowning out the tipsy haze of earlier.

AJ was instantly beside her, body low and taut, scanning the mist. "Nice," he muttered, though his hand went to her waist, steadying her. "But that's only the start."

Another figure emerged from the darkness, taller, faster. Scarlett jabbed, hooked, and spun as she'd practiced in Box Fit, but her small frame betrayed her. Strong hands grabbed her, yanking her back. She twisted, shoved, elbowed—anything—but escape felt impossible.

"Scarlett!" AJ's voice cut through the mist, calm but urgent.

In the next heartbeat, he was there, tackling the man holding her and dragging her out of reach. Breathing hard, she pressed herself against him, heart hammering, trying to steady her panic. She couldn't stop the adrenaline from racing through her veins. A third figure lunged. Scarlett ducked and jabbed with every ounce of strength she had, but AJ's grip pulled her behind him. She pressed close, heart hammering.

AJ moved like liquid, spinning into the nearest attacker. Elbows, knees, wrist locks—all precise, brutal. Scarlett caught a flicker of steel in the mist, then the man crumpled silently to the ground.

AJ muttered under his breath, barely audible: "Shit… lethal force wasn't authorised."

Scarlett froze, mind racing. What? Why would he say that? Did he just…? Her pulse thundered. The mix of fear, awe, and a tiny thrill twisted in her chest.

More figures emerged, knives glinting in the dim mist. Scarlett jabbed, hooked, and ducked as best she could, but she was small and fast—but not strong enough to fight them all off. Another set of hands grabbed her from behind, yanking her toward the underbrush. She thrashed, heart pounding, muscles screaming.

AJ spun back, taking down another attacker with brutal efficiency. Scarlett barely had time to catch her breath as he dove forward, intercepting a knife-wielding man before he could strike her. Her body pressed against his back as he fought, and adrenaline burned through her like fire. Another blade flashed near her side, cutting shallow through her jacket. Scarlett gasped, heart in her throat, but she shoved, kicked, and twisted with every scrap of training she'd learned. Her fists connected; she felt the small triumph in her hits, even as AJ continued taking the blows meant for her.

Then, chaos exploded at the edge of the clearing. Someone grabbed Scarlett from behind, spinning her around. She kicked, screamed, elbowed—but her petite frame gave her little leverage. Her heart lurched. This is bad. So bad.

AJ's voice ripped through the air. "Scarlett!"

He dove, tackling the man holding her. The sound of a struggle, knives scraping against tree trunks, and muffled grunts filled the air. AJ's movements were lethal, fluid—scarily precise. Scarlett could only cling, breathe, and pray he got her out alive. Finally, he landed with her pressed behind him, chest to chest.

His arm wrapped around her, a protective shield, as he scanned the shadows for the next threat.

"Keep close," he muttered. "They're organized… and they're not done."

Scarlett leaned against him, adrenaline and fear still thrumming through her. Her body trembled—not from weakness, but from the intensity of the fight, the closeness, the danger. She didn't know how they were going to get out, but she knew one thing: she wasn't letting go of him. Not now. Not ever. And the shadows were closing in.

Chapter 15: The Betrayal

Scarlett ran, gripping AJ's hand tightly as the mist swallowed them. Every footfall sent her heart hammering in her chest. The adrenaline from the fight in the clearing had barely worn off, and now every shadow seemed alive, every rustle a threat.

Her heel caught on a root. She stumbled, yelped, and let go of AJ's hand. Instantly, strong arms clamped around her, yanking her backward. She flailed, swinging her fists in pure panic, but her petite frame was no match for the men who had grabbed her. A sharp blow to her ribs made her gasp. Another hand smashed against her shoulder. Darkness edged her vision.

"Easy there, little firecracker," a low voice sneered in her ear. "You're far from home now."

Scarlett twisted, trying to land a punch, and connected one squarely with the side of her captor's jaw. He snarled, stumbling back. Another jab caught her stomach, and she doubled over, gasping. Her hands flew to cover her face as a boot connected with her side, knocking the wind from her.

Through the mist, a voice—or maybe a hallucination—made her freeze. "Scarlett…" it whispered, low and familiar. Uncle Gary? No. It had to be her imagination. She'd known him for years, Jade's eccentric, unpredictable uncle—the one who often tried to sell her drugs, and whom she had just seen dancing manically nearby. Could he really be here? Or was the darkness playing tricks on her?

A hand clamped over her mouth, muffling a scream. The men laughed, crude and mocking. "Struggle all you like, doll. Makes it fun." One reached for her corset, tugging at the laces. Scarlett twisted violently, swinging her elbow into his ribs. He grunted, but another grabbed her arms, pinning her to the ground. "You think you're tough?" another hissed, leering down at her. "We'll see how long that lasts." Scarlett's jaw worked as she fought to breathe. The sting of punches, the slam of boots, the sharp edge of their knives glinting in the weak dawn light—it all made her skin crawl.

Her mind spun. AJ had been right there just moments ago… hadn't he? Where was he now? The thought wormed in, insidious: maybe he'd left her. After only a week… could he really just leave her here? Doubt slithered in, sharp and bitter. He didn't really love her, did he?

The men dragged her toward a small clearing, the fire in a barrel casting twisted shadows across three looming shipping containers. Scarlett's head lolled from side to side, trying to make sense of the scene. One of the men sneered, running a hand along her arm. "Look at you… jeans and corset. Pretty little thing." His words were crude, filled with implications she refused to dwell on. She spat, trying to keep her voice defiant. "You'll have to do better than that." They laughed. One raised a fist and slammed it against her temple. Stars exploded behind her eyes, and she collapsed, momentarily dazed. Her vision swirled with mist, firelight, and the grinning, brutish faces of her captors. Another swung, connecting with her side. Scarlett's Box Fit reflexes kicked in—she twisted, shoved, and swung her legs out, catching one man with a sharp kick. He stumbled, and she bit down hard on his forearm. The taste of blood and the sharp pain in her jaw did nothing to dampen her fury. But more hands grabbed her, pinning her, knocking her to the ground again. "Not so cocky now," a voice sneered. "We're just getting started."

Scarlett's stomach churned. The taunts, the crude laughter, the pressing weight of bodies—it all coiled her nerves into a tight, vibrating spring. She refused to give them the satisfaction of terror on her face, but panic edged every thought. Her head throbbed. Her chest heaved. And somewhere in the shadows, the faint whisper of a familiar voice made her shiver again. She struggled. She kicked. She tried to pull free—but the men's coordination was seamless, methodical, practiced. Something far bigger than she could understand was at play. This wasn't just a simple capture. And through it all, Scarlett's eyes scanned the darkness, searching for AJ. He couldn't have just… left her, could he? The night stretched on, the dark mist curling like a living thing around her. Every slap, every kick, every cruel taunt hammered home the terrifying reality: she was alone.

Chapter 15: The Betrayal
Scarlett ran, gripping AJ's hand tightly as the mist swallowed them. Every footfall sent her heart hammering in her chest. The adrenaline from the fight in the clearing had barely worn off, and now every shadow seemed alive, every rustle a threat.

Her heel caught on a root. She stumbled, yelped, and let go of AJ's hand. Instantly, strong arms clamped around her, yanking her backward. She flailed, swinging her fists in pure panic, but her petite frame was no match for the men who had grabbed her. A sharp blow to her ribs made her gasp. Another hand smashed against her shoulder. Darkness edged her vision.

"Easy there, little firecracker," a low voice sneered in her ear. "You're far from home now."

Scarlett twisted, trying to land a punch, and connected one squarely with the side of her captor's jaw. He snarled, stumbling back. Another jab caught her stomach, and she doubled over, gasping. Her hands flew to cover her face as a boot connected with her side, knocking the wind from her.

Through the mist, a voice—or maybe a hallucination—made her freeze. "Scarlett…" it whispered, low and familiar. Uncle Gary? No. It had to be her imagination. She'd known him for years, Jade's eccentric, unpredictable uncle—the one who often tried to sell her drugs, and whom she had just seen dancing manically nearby. Could he really be here? Or was the darkness playing tricks on her?

A hand clamped over her mouth, muffling a scream. The men laughed, crude and mocking. "Struggle all you like, doll. Makes it fun." One reached for her corset, tugging at the laces. Scarlett twisted violently, swinging her elbow into his ribs. He grunted, but another grabbed her arms, pinning her to the ground. "You think you're tough?" another hissed, leering down at her. "We'll see how long that lasts." Scarlett's jaw worked as she fought to breathe. The sting of punches, the slam of boots, the sharp edge of their knives glinting in the weak dawn light—it all made her skin crawl.

Her mind spun. AJ had been right there just moments ago… hadn't he? Where was he now? The thought wormed in, insidious: maybe he'd left her. After only a week… could he really just leave her here? Doubt slithered in, sharp and bitter. He didn't really love her, did he?

The men dragged her toward a small clearing, the fire in a barrel casting twisted shadows across three looming shipping containers. Scarlett's head lolled from side to side, trying to make sense of the scene. One of the men sneered, running a hand along her arm. "Look at you… jeans and corset. Pretty little thing." His words were crude, filled with implications she refused to dwell on. She spat, trying to keep her voice defiant. "You'll have to do better than that." They laughed. One raised a fist and slammed it against her temple. Stars exploded behind her eyes, and she collapsed, momentarily dazed. Her vision swirled with mist, firelight, and the grinning, brutish faces of her captors. Another swung, connecting with her side. Scarlett's Box Fit reflexes kicked in—she twisted, shoved, and swung her legs out, catching one man with a sharp kick. He stumbled, and she bit down hard on his forearm. The taste of blood and the sharp pain in her jaw did nothing to dampen her fury. But more hands grabbed her, pinning her, knocking her to the ground again. "Not so cocky now," a voice sneered. "We're just getting started."

Scarlett's stomach churned. The taunts, the crude laughter, the pressing weight of bodies—it all coiled her nerves into a tight, vibrating spring. She refused to give them the satisfaction of terror on her face, but panic edged every thought. Her head throbbed. Her chest heaved. And somewhere in the shadows, the faint whisper of a familiar voice made her shiver again. She struggled. She kicked. She tried to pull free—but the men's coordination was seamless, methodical, practiced. Something far bigger than she could understand was at play. This wasn't just a simple capture. And through it all, Scarlett's eyes scanned the darkness, searching for AJ. He couldn't have just… left her, could he? The night stretched on, the dark mist curling like a living thing around her. Every slap, every kick, every cruel taunt hammered home the terrifying reality: she was alone.

Chapter 16: The Rescue Shot (TW: Violence)

Scarlett hit the ground hard. Her cheek smashed against cold mud, the force knocking a gasp from her lungs. Hands—too many of them—gripped her ribs, her thighs, her arms. She twisted violently, trying to break free, but they were coordinated. Brutal. And she was already battered from the chase.

"Hold her still," one snarled.

A knee pressed into her spine. Another into her stomach. She choked on a scream. Her vision blurred, the fire from the oil drum casting everything in a hellish, dancing glow. The three shipping containers loomed over them, their metal walls streaked with rust and graffiti. Dawn was hours off; the darkness felt endless.

One of the men crouched beside her, grinning wide enough to show missing teeth. He flicked a knife open with a careless, practiced snap.

Scarlett froze. "No," she rasped, voice shaking. "Don't—"

"Oh, we're gonna have fun," he murmured, dragging the cold blade along the top seam of her corset. "Pretty little thing like you? Dressed like you want attention."

Scarlett spat straight into his face. The reaction was immediate—a vicious slap across her cheek. Her ears rang. "You little bitch."

He grabbed the top of her corset and sliced. The blade tore downward, ripping through fabric with an ugly screech. The metal kissed her skin, then bit deeper. Scarlett screamed as the knife sliced a jagged line across her stomach—hot, sharp pain blooming instantly. Blood welled, warm against the cold night.

"Stop moving," another laughed, pinning her legs. Her corset peeled open, leaving her in only a strapless bra, her skin exposed to the freezing air and the hungry eyes above her. She tried to kick again, but hands clamped onto her ankles. Someone yanked her jeans down to her knees, forcing her legs apart. Scarlett's heart slammed in her chest—terror, fury, disbelief all colliding. *AJ... where are you?* He had been right there. She felt him holding her hand. And then—nothing. The doubt twisted inside her like barbed wire. After only a week… maybe he didn't care enough to stay. Maybe he was running for his own life. Maybe—

A hand gripped her chin, jerking her head up. "You look scared now," the attacker sneered, his body shifting on top of hers. "Good. That's the part I like." Scarlett thrashed wildly, every muscle screaming. She twisted her hips despite the pain, trying to buck him off. He laughed, grabbing both her wrists and pinning them above her head. "Keep fighting," he breathed. "Makes it better." His free hand reached down, tugging at his belt buckle. Scarlett's chest tightened. A sob ripped out of her throat. "Don't—please—" The knife man leaned in, breath sour. "No one's coming for you, princess." Scarlett's mind raced. She clawed at the dirt, at anything, but she was trapped under his weight, her jeans down, blood dripping from her stomach wound, her voice breaking—*AJ isn't coming. He left. He left me. He actually—*

BANG. The roar of the gunshot split the clearing. The man on top of her convulsed. His eyes widened in shock. For a suspended heartbeat, nothing moved. Then he collapsed—dead weight—onto her chest.

Scarlett screamed beneath him. The body was rolled off her with one brutal shove. And then AJ was there. His face wasn't calm now. It was carved from steel—terrifying, focused, lethal. He held a handgun in both hands, stance locked, breath controlled. Scarlett barely recognized him.

Two attackers remained. Both lunged. "Scarlett, STAY DOWN!" he barked. She tried. Her body shook uncontrollably. Blood trickled from the cut across her stomach. Her jeans were still down, her corset shredded, the cold gnawing at her exposed skin—but all she could do was crawl backward, scrambling away from the dead man's outstretched hand.

The first attacker swung a knife at AJ's face. AJ ducked, grabbed the man's wrist, twisted—CRACK. A yelp of agony. The knife clattered to the ground. AJ didn't hesitate. He shot him once in the chest. The man collapsed instantly. The final attacker let out a panicked curse and charged. AJ blocked the first punch, but the second hit him across the jaw. A third blow landed in his ribs. AJ staggered, catching himself on one knee. Scarlett's heart lurched. "No—AJ—!" The attacker grabbed AJ by the collar, lifting the knife. AJ moved like a whip. A sharp elbow to the ribs. A slam of his palm into the man's throat. The attacker gagged, stumbling back—and AJ fired. The man dropped.

Silence.

Scarlett sat trembling, half-undressed, bleeding, her breath coming in ragged, painful gasps. The world tilted. The fire crackled. Her stomach burned. She pulled her jeans up shakily, but her hands couldn't stop shaking long enough to fasten them. AJ kicked the last body away and rushed to her. "Scarlett—Scarlett, look at me." He dropped to his knees beside her, hands cupping her face gently despite the blood smeared across his knuckles. She stared up at him, tears welling uncontrollably. "You… you came." His voice broke, soft but firm. "Of course I came." She let out a sob, collapsing into him. His arms wrapped around her instantly, fiercely, protectively. His warmth shielded her shaking body, his breath brushing her hair. "I thought you left me," she whispered. "I thought you'd gone." "Never," AJ growled, pulling her tighter. "Not a chance." Scarlett buried her face in his chest, crying softly as he held her against him. Her stomach wound stung with every breath. Her ribs throbbed. She felt bruised everywhere. She clung to him, shaking violently. AJ glanced at her injuries and swore under his breath. "We need to get you out of here. Now." Scarlett nodded weakly, her voice cracking, "My… my cat—Jonesy—" "I'll get him," AJ promised immediately. "You're not going home tonight. It's not safe. They have your phone. They know your address." She blinked at him, dizzy. "They took my phone?" "Yes." His jaw clenched. "Which means we're not risking it. You're coming with me." She nodded, her strength fading as shock crept in. "Ok," she whispered. AJ lifted her gently into his arms. And Scarlett let herself go limp against his chest.

Chapter 17: Detective Sergeant Arthur Jacobs

Scarlett woke slowly—thick-headed, aching everywhere, wrapped in warmth that didn't belong to her. Soft fabric brushed her cheek. A duvet. Clean. Heavy. Expensive. And beneath her… a mattress. Not hers. Too big. Too soft. Her eyes cracked open. She was in a bed. AJ's bed. The room was bright with pale November morning light, spilling through tall windows onto dark wood floors. Everything was neat—precision neat. A wardrobe with military corners, shelves lined with books and framed photos. No clutter. No chaos.

Scarlett's heart thudded painfully. A slow, creeping memory surfaced—the attack, the knife, the hands pinning her down, the gunshot, AJ's arms around her as everything faded. Her breathing quickened. She pushed herself upright with a hiss, hand flying to her ribs. Pain flared sharp enough to make her vision flicker. Beneath the duvet was one of AJ's T-shirts hanging off her like a dress—all she had on. Her skin prickled with humiliation she hated herself for.

Before she could panic, a deep voice came from the doorway. "You're awake."

Scarlett jerked her head up. AJ stood there—still in the same black clothes as hours before, dried mud on his boots, knuckles scraped, a faint bruise darkening his jaw. His eyes softened the second they met hers. Relief, raw and unfiltered.

"Scarlett," he breathed. "Thank God." He stepped in slowly, hands raised slightly—like approaching a frightened animal.

"Where am I?" she whispered.

"My house," he said gently. "You're safe."

Safe. The word made something inside her tilt, then crack. But before the anger could surge, he spoke again—quiet but firm. "I need to tell you who I actually am."

Scarlett froze. AJ exhaled once, steadying himself. "My name is still AJ… but my full name is Detective Sergeant Arthur Jacobs. Covert operations. Specialist Crime."

Her stomach flipped violently. "You're… police?"

He nodded once.

"And you used me?" Her voice was a whisper of betrayal.

"No." He walked closer, slowly. "Scarlett, you were never part of the operation. Never a target. Never a tool. You got caught in it because I—" He stopped, jaw tightening. "Because I cared about you more than I should've. And I should've protected you better."

"You lied to me."

"I had to," he said softly. "But not about us."

"If I'd known what you were… I'd never have gone into those woods. Never."

"I know," he said. "And that's why I didn't tell you. Not because I didn't trust you — because you'd have run. And I couldn't risk losing sight of you in that chaos."

"Was anything real?" she whispered.

"Everything with you was real," AJ said instantly. "All of it."

He stepped closer and sat on the edge of the bed. "You're injured. You need rest. I cleaned the cuts on your stomach and ribs, but they'll need looking at again later. And your concussion—"

"My cat," Scarlett blurted suddenly, panic flaring fresh. "Jonesy. He's been alone all night. He'll be going feral—he hates being ignored—"

"I know," AJ said softly.

"You know?"

He gave a tiny, tired smile. "Ginger lunatic who tries to attack my shoelaces every time I walk into your bedroom? Hard to forget."

Despite everything, Scarlett almost laughed. "I need him, AJ."

"I know." He touched her hand gently. "I'll get him."

"When?" she whispered.

"Now."

"How will you get in? Do you even know where I keep the key?" she asked, worry etching her voice.

"I do," he said quietly, with a look that made her chest ache. "I've stayed at yours twice. I know your house. I know the broken step on the stairs. I know the mug you always use. I know how you fall asleep on your side with your hand under the pillow." His voice dropped. "I know you, Scarlett."

"And I'll bring him here," he promised. "You're not going home. It's not safe. They took your phone — they could track you. We'll get you a new one today. I'll help you call work on Monday. Car accident is believable."

As he stood to leave, sunlight caught a series of photos on his shelf. She saw him in army fatigues, medals pinned neatly to his chest, and then two children in his arms.

"Those are my niece and nephew," he said softly, catching her gaze. "My sister's kids."

"AJ?"

"Yeah?"

"Before you go… can I have a cup of tea? Please?"

His expression softened completely. "Course you can." A pause. "Yorkshire or Tetley?"

A tiny laugh escaped her chest despite everything. "Yorkshire. Obviously."

He gave the faintest smile. "Good girl."

And then he disappeared toward the kitchen, leaving her in his bed — wounded, furious, terrified, confused… and falling for a man who had just blown her entire world apart.

Chapter 18: Bleeding and Protocol

Scarlett sat cross-legged on the floor, knees stiff, every muscle in her body complaining. The kettle's warmth from the tea AJ had made moments ago seeped into her hands, grounding her, giving her a tiny sense of control. She finally let herself inspect her wounds. The butterfly stitches over her stomach itched faintly beneath the bandages, a harsh reminder of the blade that had sliced through her corset. Her ribs ached when she breathed deeply, the bruises blossoming purple beneath her skin.

She traced a cautious finger over the bandaged slice on her stomach, taking care not to disturb the fragile stitches. Her gaze flicked to the room, scanning AJ's house again. She spotted a photo of him shaking hands with a fellow soldier. Another frame showed him with two children, laughing in the garden, sunlight catching his hair. For a moment, she let herself imagine normality.

A soft click made her whip around. The front door had closed. AJ stumbled into the living room, one arm pressed to his side, the other retrieving something from a hidden trouser pocket. He held a terrified but familiar ball of ginger fur: Jonesy.

Scarlett gasped. "Jonesy!"

"Scarlett," he rasped, ignoring the cat as he moved carefully. "I… I need to call Deedee. Protocol."

He crouched beside the sofa, careful not to put weight on his shoulder which was bleeding. She noticed the dark stain spreading across his black shirt, her stomach tightening. His breathing was shallow but steady. AJ reached into the hidden pocket, pulling out his phone.

"House secure?" he asked, eyes flicking to her.

She nodded, still tense. "Yes… for now."

He scrolled quickly, calling a secure number. "Yes, it's me. Situation at the house," he said, his voice clipped and efficient. "Deedee? I'm injured... minor, but bleeding. Scarlett is here. Safe. The immediate threat is neutralized."

Scarlett's eyes widened slightly at the mention of the name she recognized from that suspicious early morning call. She patched up the fresh bleeding spots as best she could, dabbing and pressing, making sure the wound was contained, the pressure consistent. Her hands trembled, but she forced her movements steady.

Through it all, Jonesy padded nervously around them, curling at her feet occasionally, clearly sensing the tension. Scarlett reached down, stroking the ginger fur, taking solace in the little creature's presence.

AJ finally leaned back against the sofa. "They're sending instructions... containment... extraction... only if safe," he said, voice quieter now, almost to himself. He met her gaze for the first time since entering the room. "Scarlett… I need you to stay calm. Don't move, don't leave. Let me… rest."

Scarlett sank to the floor beside him. "We'll figure this out," she whispered to herself, more than to him. "We have to." And she knew, deep down, that whatever came next, she would not leave him. Not again.

Chapter 19: British Tapas

The living room was bathed in the warm, golden glow of early evening. It was the soft, muted light of a Sunday afternoon, utterly belying the sheer violence that had happened less than twelve hours earlier. Scarlett lay sprawled on the carpet, wrapped tightly in a thick wool blanket, her back pressed against AJ's side. His arm was draped protectively over her, a warm, heavy weight that felt like an anchor. Jonesy, the ginger cat, having finished his initial nervous exploration of the strange new house, padded carefully around them, sniffing and circling, before settling in a tight, protective curl close to AJ's legs.

The silence was the deepest kind of comfort, broken only by the crackle of the fireplace—a luxury Scarlett's terrace house lacked. She could hear the slow, steady rhythm of AJ's breathing, a contrast to the frantic, ragged gasps they had shared in the clearing.

AJ shifted carefully, easing Scarlett slightly so he could rise. Every movement was controlled, betraying his military training, yet a flicker of pain crossed his face as he put weight on his shoulder. "I should… get up," he muttered, his voice rough but controlled. "Can't leave Jonesy like this. Needs a proper setup."

He eased himself upright, wincing only slightly at the tension in his shoulder, which was now tightly bandaged beneath his T-shirt. "I'll be careful," he insisted, catching her worried look. "I stopped at the shop before coming here—picked up a cheap litter tray, litter, and some food. At least the basics." He managed a small, tired smile. "I also grabbed essentials. Don't worry, the Aldi is well-stocked for a covert mission."

He moved around the kitchen with practiced economy, navigating the space easily despite his bruised shoulder. Scarlett watched him, fascinated by the precise, almost minimalist organization of his home. Every spice jar was aligned, every tool put away. It was the home of a man who lived in a permanent state of readiness.

"Fancy dinner?" he asked, nodding toward the fridge.

Scarlett raised an eyebrow, adjusting the blanket around her ribs. "I assumed dinner meant tea and painkillers. You managed to find actual food?"

He smirked, voice rough but soft. "Oh, I found food. We're having British tapas."

She blinked. "What the... what the fuck is that?"

"It's my version of tapas," he explained, pulling out a bag of frozen chips, a leftover pork pie, and a packet of chicken nuggets. "Bits of what I like—pie, chicken nuggets, chips… all together. Simple, satisfying. British style. It's the kind of food that requires zero mental energy, which is exactly what we need right now."

Scarlett laughed, a sound lighter than it had been all week. The sheer, unpretentious charm of the meal—or lack thereof—was a shock after the intense formality of the last few hours. "Seriously? That's your idea of tapas?"

"Yep. Works for me. Works for hungry people," he said, already preheating the oven with efficient movements. "Don't worry, it tastes better than it sounds. It's comfort food with zero risk of nutritional complexity."

As they ate the haphazard meal—AJ leaning against the counter, she perched on a stool—the casual nature of the scene felt intensely profound. The grease, the laughter, the sound of the oven timer—it was all deeply domestic, a defiant rejection of the brutality that had stalked them.

After they finished the last of the chips, AJ finally turned his attention to his own deeper injuries. "Right," he said, pulling a first-aid kit from under the sink. "I need to properly dress this shoulder before it gets worse."

While he worked methodically, wrapping his shoulder with the clinical precision of someone who had done this many times before, he spoke in the clipped, professional tone of Detective Sergeant Jacobs. "Tomorrow, we report to my unit. I have to explain everything—your involvement, our… relationship. There'll be questions, warnings. Consequences. I'll take my lashes, metaphorical or otherwise, but your account needs to be solid."

He met her gaze, his dark eyes serious. "You'll be asked about the attack, the exchange we saw in the woods, and why you were there. We stick to the car accident story for your job, but for the unit, we stick to the truth about the rave and the violence. I'll handle the rest."

AJ finally stood, stretching carefully, his tall frame easing the stiffness out of his body. He held out a hand, his expression softening entirely. "Come on. Bed. You're not sleeping on the floor tonight."

In the bedroom, there was no rush. AJ was gentle, patient. They moved slowly, exploring closeness rather than urgency, healing the trauma of the night with quiet intimacy and trust. Afterward, Scarlett rested in his arms, feeling the steady beat of his heart against her ear. "You're ridiculous," she whispered, thinking of the pie and the pop-punk.

AJ chuckled softly, pulling the duvet higher around her neck. "And terrifying. Don't forget that."

Chapter 20: The Black Parade and the Cornflakes

AJ's alarm exploded into life at exactly 7 am. Scarlett jerked upright, hair wild, heart hammering—a residual echo from the violence of the night before. She expected a military bugle or perhaps a coded police alert, but instead, she froze as the sound registered. Blink-182. "First Date." The upbeat, ridiculously nostalgic pop-punk anthem was blaring from the bedside table.

She stared at AJ, incredulous, the duvet slipping down to her waist. "You listen to Blink-182?"

He cracked one eye open, the bruise on his jaw looking dark and painful in the morning light. "Don't judge me before coffee," he mumbled, his voice gravelly from sleep and exhaustion. He reached out and silenced the alarm, but the moment was set. His defensive tone quickly gave way to a grudging smile. "It's good morning music. Gets the circulation going."

He didn't wait for her retort. He switched the playlist on his phone. The opening, dramatic piano notes of My Chemical Romance's "Welcome to the Black Parade" hit the room like a physical punch. Scarlett gasped, forgetting her aches and injuries for a second. "No fucking way. Detective Sergeant Arthur Jacobs listens to MCR?"

"Oh yes," he said, sitting up straighter, the simple action making him wince slightly as he moved his bruised shoulder. "We're doing this."

What followed was an impromptu, whispered karaoke session as they desperately tried to remember all the lyrics to the epic anthem. They reached for notes they couldn't hit, mumbled through verses they'd forgotten, and used exaggerated gestures for the marching band sections. By the time they reached the powerful, soaring climax—"We'll carry on, we'll carry on!"—both of them were laughing so hard she had tears streaming down her face.

The absurdity of the situation—two people who had spent less than a week in each other's lives, who had just survived a brutal ambush and was now caught in covert police protocol, singing angsty 2000s rock—was a sudden, overwhelming release. It was a shared vulnerability that bypassed the need for formal confessions or lengthy explanations, solidifying their bizarre, intense bond more effectively than any conversation could.

When the laughter finally subsided, leaving the room quiet and smelling faintly of adrenaline and sleep, AJ checked the time. The transition back to duty was immediate, the playful DJ vanishing, replaced by the methodical Detective Sergeant. "It's nearly seven-thirty. We need to be at my unit by nine."

Scarlett felt a jolt of anxiety. "I don't have any clothes. Like… at all," she gestured helplessly, acutely aware she was only wearing his oversized T-shirt.

AJ's gaze swept over her—a quick, professional assessment that nonetheless held residual warmth. "I can lend you stuff. My T-shirts are long enough to cover your bum and my sports shorts have a drawstring—so they'll stay on your tiny, weirdly compact solicitor body." He used the technical term "solicitor body" with a dry humour that made her smile.

Five minutes later she emerged, having struggled into his borrowed clothes. The T-shirt pooled around her, and the shorts were a voluminous disaster cinched tight at the waist. AJ took one look, barked a laugh, and pointed at her with a spatula, which she hadn't noticed him pick up. "You look like Vincent in Pulp Fiction when he has to borrow the emergency clothes and ends up looking like he's doing punishment PE."

"Coffee?" AJ asked, moving toward the kitchen, his morning routine already kicking in.

"Yes. All of it. Strong enough to kill a spider."

A minute later he paused mid-reach into the cupboard, holding a plain cardboard box. He turned, looking genuinely nervous for the first time since confessing his identity. "Please don't judge me for this." He held up… a box of Aldi own-brand cornflakes.

She laughed harder, clutching the edge of the counter for support. "Aldi is elite. Are you kidding? You go in for a loaf of bread and come out with a two-man tent and a saxophone. What's not to love about that chaotic brilliance?"

AJ snorted so violently he had to put the cereal down on the counter. His shoulders shook with silent laughter. "Okay, yeah, fair. I think that's the most accurate description of the experience I've ever heard."

The moment, small as it was—sharing a cheap breakfast in borrowed clothes after surviving an attempted kidnapping—felt overwhelmingly right. She saw not just the dangerous cop or the mysterious DJ, but a man who was endearingly thrifty, a secret pop-punk fan, and someone who saw her own chaotic nature and simply laughed. This was the man who had just saved her life, and now he was offering her the safest possible chaos she could imagine.

Chapter 21: Nine O'Clock Protocol

The bowls were empty on the kitchen counter, remnants of their "British tapas" spread a final layer of absurd domesticity over the chaos they had survived. Scarlett sat back, stretching carefully to avoid pulling the stitches, the borrowed T-shirt falling slightly off one shoulder, and gave AJ a sideways grin.

"Vincent Vega," he teased again, using the film reference as a shared, comforting shorthand for the impossible situation they were in.

The brief moment of levity dissolved as AJ stood, retrieving his car keys. His expression was once again shuttered, the professional mask firmly back in place. He slid into the driver's seat of his sleek black car—which looked less like a tree surgeon's vehicle and more like government issue—and motioned for her to buckle up.

Scarlett pulled the belt across her bruised ribs and spoke before the silence could become too heavy. "I…"

she began, her voice low and tight. "I need to know. That night, in the woods, when you said you loved me… you were serious, right? You weren't just using operational psychology to calm down the witness?"

He kept his eyes on the road, navigating the quiet residential streets with the same hyper-focus he'd shown in the clearing. "I meant it, Scarlett. Every word. I said it because I meant it. I couldn't just stand by. Not then, not now. I love you. Always."

The Glass Façade

The journey was short but intensely charged. The car pulled up outside the sleek glass-and-steel façade of AJ's unit. It wasn't a standard police station; it looked like a fortress of corporate anonymity, guarded by technology. Scarlett felt her legal instincts prickle, recognizing the sterile authority of the place.

Inside, the foyer was quiet, humming with an atmosphere of contained power. She followed AJ through security, past the buzz of keycards and scanning cameras. His manner was instantly transformed; his back straighter, his voice reserved, every motion communicating control. He was Detective Sergeant Arthur Jacobs now, not the chaotic DJ she'd fallen for.

They reached an inner corridor, where AJ paused, turning to her. "Remember the plan," he murmured, his gaze intense. "Car accident for the outside world. The truth for the debrief. Stick to what happened in the woods."

Before she could respond, a door opened, and a sharply dressed officer—a woman with the brisk competence of someone who dealt only in facts—appeared. "Ms. Harper? We're ready for you now."

The Debriefing Room

The air in the interview room was cold, stark with bright fluorescent lights and a large, empty table that magnified the tension. Two other officers sat there, folders open, their expressions neutral and unreadable. This wasn't an interrogation room; it was a fact-finding environment, and she, the unauthorized civilian, was the key witness.

"Ms. Harper," the first officer began, her voice cool and measured. "We understand you were involved in an incident over the weekend. We need a clear account of events, from your perspective."

Though her ribs ached and her throat was dry, Scarlett drew upon her training as a solicitor. She spoke clearly, sticking to the facts she could verify. She recounted the clearing, the sudden, violent escalation, the masked men, the flash of the knife, and the terror of being pinned down. She described the chilling things she'd seen and the lethal force AJ had used to save her.

"Thank you, Ms. Harper," the first officer said finally, closing her file with a decisive snap. "That's very helpful. We may have follow-up questions, but for now, that's everything we need."

A crippling wave of exhaustion and relief washed over Scarlett. She wanted desperately to run, to escape the cold glass and steel of this place. Her eyes flicked toward the door AJ had disappeared through—the door to his own debrief. The same door that would lead to his own reckoning for involving a civilian, for using unauthorized lethal force, and for breaking every rule in the book by blurring the lines between his covert job and his personal life. She didn't know what awaited him, but a knot of dread coiled in her stomach. Their shared future, fragile and reckless, hung entirely on the next few hours.

Chapter 22: Suspension

Scarlett stepped out of the interrogation room, the sterile silence of the air-conditioned corridor a stark contrast to the floodlights and sharp questions she'd just endured. She felt hollowed out, the adrenaline and professional composure she'd relied on completely spent. Years in the courtroom had taught her to present, to control, to command attention. But here, she was the witness. Vulnerable. Exposed.

She rounded the corner, her eyes searching desperately for AJ, and froze. He was standing by the edge of the parking lot, bathed in the pale, weak afternoon sun filtering through the glass façade. He hadn't changed into civilian clothes yet; he was still in the jacket he'd worn the night before, his hands shoved deep into his pockets. But something was profoundly, terribly off. His shoulders were tighter than usual, his jaw set in a rigid line of suppressed tension, and the casual lean he usually employed was gone, replaced by a defeated slump.

"AJ…" Her voice trembled, the exhaustion finally catching up with her.

He turned slowly, his movement stiff and reluctant. "Hey," he said, his voice low, clipped, and devoid of its usual comforting resonance.

"What… what happened?" The knot of dread that had coiled in her stomach during her debriefing tightened into a cold fist.

He exhaled slowly, watching the traffic rush past. "They're… putting me on suspension. Internal investigation." He couldn't meet her eyes, instead focusing on the middle distance. "For being... with you the other night. And, well…" He paused, the difficulty of saying the words evident in the way his throat worked. "For how things went with the op. The cover was blown, three bodies were left on a disused site, and there's the use of unauthorized lethal force. I—I messed up."

Scarlett felt the ground give way beneath her. The impact of the word "suspension," and the realization of the professional gravity of his actions, hit her with stunning force. "You… what?"

"I didn't mean for any of it to happen," he insisted quickly, voice cracking a little despite his effort to keep it steady. "I thought I had it under control. I thought I could keep the operation contained while also protecting you. And I failed. Now they're suspending me while they figure out what went wrong, and whether my relationship with you compromised the operation from the start."

The gravity of the consequences was staggering. "It feels like—like I ruined everything for you. Your job, your career, everything you risked."

AJ finally looked at her, his dark eyes wide and pleading, the vulnerability exposed. "Scarlett… you saved me the other night, you really did. You don't ruin anything. You… you just make me… human." He took a small step closer, a desperate attempt to bridge the gulf the system had just created between them.

Then, almost teasing, he made a sharp shift in tone, forcing a familiar, painful lightness. "Vincent Vega, you know… still rocking the borrowed clothes look."

Scarlett couldn't help it. A small, shaky laugh escaped her lips despite everything. The visual of his large, dangerous frame in her ridiculous borrowed shorts was jarringly funny, a necessary distraction from the cold dread.

She wanted to reach out, to reassure him, to fix it all with a word or a touch. But all she could do was stand there, silent, realizing that the danger wasn't over. The threats weren't just in the dark woods anymore; they were internal, professional, and potentially career-ending. The world had shifted again, and now they were facing the fallout together.

Chapter 23: The Shattered Mug

That's an excellent point about Scarlett's immediate, practical instincts overriding her exhaustion, and AJ's protective instinct overriding his current emotional state. She wouldn't just delegate; she'd start working. He would stop her due to her injuries and the risk of the ceramic shrapnel.

I will revise the final dialogue block to reflect this more realistic interaction.

Here is Chapter 23 in full, revised for emotional and practical continuity:

The drive back to AJ's new-build was agonizingly silent, the previous morning's lighthearted Blink-182 and cornflakes feeling like a lifetime ago. The tension was a physical thing, thick and poisonous, clotting the air in the sleek black car. Scarlett couldn't bring herself to break it, the small, shaky laugh from the parking lot long forgotten. Every time she looked at AJ's profile—the faint bruise darkening on his jaw, the muscle twitching with tension around his mouth—guilt, sharp and cold, twisted in her gut. She was a witness, a casualty, yet she felt responsible for derailing his entire life.

When they finally pulled up to his house, AJ didn't move. He just rested his forearms on the steering wheel, head bowed, staring through the windscreen at the neat, anodyne street. The engine hummed for a long, torturous moment before he killed it.

"AJ?" she whispered, the quiet sound barely cutting through the manufactured silence of the car.

He exhaled a shuddering breath that wasn't a sigh—it was a fight for control, a physiological system attempting to reset and failing. "I'm sorry," he murmured, the words rough. "I know you want answers. I know you deserve them. But I… I can't right now."

Scarlett reached for his hand, tracing the faint smudges of ink on his knuckles. "You don't have to talk about the investigation, AJ. Just… talk about you."

He lifted his head, and his eyes, usually so intensely brown and sharp, looked dull, flat. Empty. It was terrifying. "My job is structure, Scarlett," he said, his voice low, clipped, and unnaturally steady. "My job is compartmentalizing chaos. I spend my life maintaining the line between us and them. I failed. I lost the line. I lost control. And they know. Every single person in that building knows." He didn't sound angry or sad. He sounded like he was reciting a post-mortem report over a dead man.

"A suspension is what they call the time it takes to fire me. The organization we were tracking—they know I'm exposed. They know I was compromised by a civilian. My career is over, Scarlett. Done."

He finally moved, shoving the car door open with more force than necessary and walking toward the house without looking back. Inside, the usual precise order of his home seemed to mock the ruin of his professional life. Jonesy padded toward them with a plaintive cry, weaving through AJ's legs, instantly sensing the immense tension. AJ didn't acknowledge him.

He walked straight to the kitchen island, his movements stiff, almost robotic. He grabbed a heavy ceramic mug—the one he always used, large and plain—and went to the tap. He filled it with water, then stared at it. For a man who was always doing something—cleaning, organizing, fixing, moving—his complete stillness was unnerving. The only sound was the soft *drip-drip-drip* of the tap he hadn't fully closed.

"AJ?"

He didn't answer. He just stood there, looking at the full mug of tap water, the silence stretching taut, brittle, and unbearable. Then, with a sudden, violent movement born of pure, systemic failure, he threw the mug at the opposite wall. It didn't shatter—it exploded. The sound was deafening, the ceramic fragments hitting the sleek, white cabinets and scattering across the dark wood floor. Water sprayed everywhere, dripping audibly from the polished surfaces. Scarlett jumped back, a small gasp escaping her lips. Jonesy, terrified, hissed and disappeared under the sofa. AJ stood frozen, his chest heaving, his immaculate kitchen suddenly a battlefield of ceramic shrapnel and dark, wet patches. The control had snapped.

He let out a choked sound—half-sob, half-growl, a noise of pure, animalistic pain—and leaned heavily against the counter, forehead pressed against the cool granite. Scarlett moved cautiously, ignoring the debris and the threat of the broken porcelain. She stopped just behind him and placed her hands gently on his back.

"It's okay, AJ," she murmured into his back. "It's okay. It's just a mug."

"I don't lose control, Scarlett. I can't. Not ever. That's the job."

"It's not your job anymore," she said quietly. "You're just AJ. And you're allowed to be angry."

"We need to talk about Jade," Scarlett said, needing to regain some control by focusing on a concrete problem. "She'll be worried. And I need to see her face to face. I can't just disappear without a word."

AJ's eyes snapped down to her. "No, Scarlett," he said, pushing off the counter, his voice raw with urgency. "Absolutely not. The men who attacked you—they were connected to the drug supply at the rave. They know you were with me. They know your house. You go near Jade, you're putting yourself, and us, right back in the path of the people who just tried to kill us. And Jade's uncle, Gary, is a dealer in that network."

"Exactly," Scarlett argued, stepping away from him to put space between them. "He tried to sell us weed last week, for God's sake—he's just a wired old dealer on the circuit, nothing more. He's harmless. Jade's the one who knows how to keep her head down in this estate; she's lived here forever. I need to see her, AJ. I need to see my friend."

"Fine," he conceded, the word tight with utter reluctance. "But we don't call. We don't announce ourselves. We go there, we assess the environment, and we leave immediately. And Scarlett," he grabbed her arms, forcing her to look at him, "you stay behind me. Every step."

"AJ, wait," she said, stopping him from moving toward the front door. "I'm an associate solicitor, specializing in family law, but I've just completed the Bar course. I understand misconduct procedures. You need professional counsel here. Let me see the paperwork from your unit."

"I'm not paying for a solicitor," he muttered, rubbing his eyes.

"Exactly, and they'll be using every piece of procedure against you," she cut in before he could object. "Your relationship with a civilian caught in the periphery of a target is the biggest liability. I need to read the basis of the suspension. At the very least, I can help you articulate your defence for the formal hearing. I owe you that."

He reached into his jacket pocket and pulled out a single, folded sheet of paper. "It's just a printed sheet. Suspension letter," he muttered. "Read it on the road."

"Fine," she said, snatching the letter from his hand, already moving toward the mess. She bent down to retrieve a large shard of ceramic near the sofa.

"Stop! Don't touch that," AJ barked, his voice immediately sharp with operational command, snapping him out of his trance. He grabbed her arm gently but firmly, pulling her away from the debris. "You're injured, and there's glass everywhere. I clean this up. You take care of yourself, and the cat."

"I'll make sure Jonesy has enough food and water then," she relented, holding the suspension letter. "And I'll read this on the way to Jade's. You clean up your crime scene."

The quiet authority in her voice finally seemed to break through his despair. He looked at the chaos he'd created, then at the small, wounded solicitor standing beside him, and slowly, stiffly, he nodded. Scarlett knew, in that moment, that if they were to survive this ruin, she couldn't just be his witness; she had to be his lawyer, his anchor, and his new source of structure.

Chapter 24: Gary's Landing

Jade lived in a council flat in the older, industrial end of the city. The buildings were concrete, utilitarian, and stacked high. "It's temporary, practical," AJ murmured, maneuvering the sleek black car into a shadowed space three blocks away. He pulled the vehicle tightly against a dilapidated warehouse wall. "Council flats are excellent for anonymity. Multiple points of entry and exit. High flow of people. No one notices a new face or a parked car for long."

They walked the final blocks in silence, the rhythm of their footsteps and the low rush of traffic the only sounds. AJ kept a steady, military pace, his suspension letter folded and tucked securely into his jacket. Scarlett clutched the same jacket sleeve, feeling the bandage on her stomach pull with every step. When they reached Jade's block, a large, grimy structure of reinforced concrete, AJ stopped her behind a huge, overflowing skip. The stench of refuse and stale food was overwhelming, but the shadow was deep.

"Stay here," he instructed, his voice low and serious. "I go first. I check the stairwell. I check her landing. If anything feels off, we abort, no questions."

He moved swiftly, disappearing into the dark maw of the main entrance. Scarlett leaned against the skip, trying to slow her hammering heart, the five agonizing minutes he was gone feeling like an hour. When AJ's head finally reappeared at the ground floor entrance, he gave a tiny, almost imperceptible nod. "Clear."

She followed him inside. The air in the stairwell was cold and smelled of old smoke and cheap cleaner. They climbed five flights, the sound of their soft-soled shoes echoing slightly on the worn linoleum steps. When they reached the fifth-floor landing, AJ paused again, his ears straining against the thin music leaking from behind a door. "Normal," he reported, the observation precise. He then knocked three times—a simple, deliberate rhythm.

Jade opened the door instantly, her face pale, eyes wide and red-rimmed. She was wearing yesterday's clothes, and it was clear she hadn't slept. "Scar! Oh my god, you absolute idiot! Where the hell have you been?!"

Jade gripped her so tightly that Scarlett's bruised ribs screamed in protest, but the pain was instantly dulled by the massive wave of relief flooding her system. "I'm sorry, Jade. I'm okay. I lost my clothes and my phone."

Then Jade's gaze landed on AJ. The protective instincts of a loyal best friend flared, instantly bypassing her exhaustion. "Right. And who the hell is this?" She planted herself between them. "The DJ? From the woods rave? What did you do to her?"

"She's fine. Just rough," AJ intervened smoothly, keeping his voice level. He stepped past Jade, putting himself at Scarlett's side. "I was there, I heard she was in trouble. I came to help. I'm AJ."

Scarlett pushed past them both into the warm, scented air of the flat. "Shut up, both of you. I need a bath, a massive cup of tea, and to borrow some clothes that don't make me look like I'm doing community service."

Jade ushered them inside. The flat was small, comfortable chaos—old furniture, brightly coloured throws, and a general messiness that spoke of real, lived-in life. Then Scarlett froze.

In the small, cluttered living room, sat an enormous, cream-coloured leather sofa—the kind that screamed cash job and was spectacularly out of place in a council flat. And on that sofa, sitting stiffly, was Gary.

He was wearing an over-stretched, fluorescent green vest and patched jeans, his pupils dilated wide enough to be completely black, even in the modest light. He was fiddling with a complex, small electronic device—a soldering iron and circuit board laid out on a folded towel.

"Scarlett!" Gary gurned, his voice unnervingly cheerful. "We thought you'd gone off-grid! Heard you had a bit of a rumble in the woods, eh? Lost your phone?" His eyes slid past her, landing on AJ. The smile never wavered, but the black pin-prick pupils narrowed sharply as he processed the man standing in his home.

"And you brought the music man!" Gary cackled, a manic, high-pitched sound. "Arthur, my man, how's the leg? Running from the fuzz can be a killer on the tendons!" Gary hadn't been expecting them. But the chilling fact that he knew AJ's full name, *Arthur,* and was aware of AJ's minor injury sustained during the rave's escape (Chapter 2) meant the calculation had already begun behind his manic eyes. This wasn't a harmless old dealer; this was a man with deep connections, and they were walking straight into his base.

Chapter 25: The Network Commander

The silence that fell was thick and hot, broken only by the faint, menacing hiss of the soldering iron Gary was working with. The air in the cluttered living room was now charged with hostility.

"Scarlett," Gary gurned, his eyes flicking over her bruised face and borrowed clothes. "You're shaking like a shitting dog, darling. You need a hit. Arthur, my man, how about you stand guard and I fix these poor kids up? I've got a new skunk—absolute dynamite. Special batch."

AJ stood rigid, a dark anchor in the room's chaotic bright colours. He was ignoring the drug offer, ignoring the threat, and ignoring the use of his formal name. "Jade," AJ stated, his voice steady but low, addressing the only truly neutral person. "We need a towelling robe for Scarlett and some antiseptic. She needs to clean her wounds."

Gary laughed, a dry, grating sound. "Wounds! See? Always dramatic, you kids. Arthur here is just trying to look after his little solicitor, Jade, bless." Gary pointed the soldering iron at AJ, not as a tool but as a bizarre, searing weapon. "Tell me, Arthur, how did you get such a nasty knock on the shoulder? Was it running from the pigs at the first rave? You moved pretty fast that night, didn't you?"

"It was a chainsaw accident," AJ repeated, his voice flat, maintaining the long-dead cover story.

"A chains— rubbish," Gary snorted, dismissing the lie instantly. "You haven't got a scratch on your neck. No sawdust in your hair. You move like a ghost. You move like someone who's been trained to clear a room in under sixty seconds, Arthur. Tree surgeons don't move like that." The casual, drug-fueled façade had completely dropped, revealing a razor-sharp, chilling intelligence underneath.

Gary lifted his hand, gesturing with the soldering iron, tracing the history of their brief acquaintance. "When you disappeared mid-set at the first rave, the lads were told to check your DJ booth. They didn't find anything unusual, but they did notice you were gone the second the lights came on. And you didn't sprint with the rest of the mugs; you went quietly into the shadows. You didn't run like a raver, Arthur. You ran like someone who knew the perimeter, the escape routes, and the timing of the raid."

He paused for dramatic effect, his eyes boring into AJ. "You were scanning the crowd before the music cut. You were waiting for the signal. You were the police informant that shut down our night."

Jade let out a small, choked sound, her hand flying to her mouth. The betrayal, the shock, and the reality of their dangerous proximity were written instantly on her face. AJ's cover was gone, irrevocably shattered in the space of three sentences. Scarlett felt her stomach turn over, realizing the depth of the deception and the danger they were now in.

"We got the phone your solicitor friend lost during the scramble. We found her address, and more importantly, we found the texts from your police burner confirming you were compromised. We sent the lads to verify you, and Michael confirmed you were personally involved." Gary stepped past the sofa, moving deliberately and purposefully. "You know what Michael told me, Arthur? He said you didn't just defend her. You were angry. You were protective. You were personally compromised. That's a weakness, copper. And you brought that weakness straight to my niece's flat. Now, what do you suggest we do?"

AJ took a sharp, controlled step back, shielding Scarlett entirely with his body, every muscle tight. "You let us walk out of here. You never see us again."

Gary threw his head back and laughed, a genuine, manic burst of amusement. "Oh, Arthur. That's not how the bassline works. Once you're in the mix, you're in the mix forever. I think you need a place to reflect on your failures."

Chapter 26: The Boarded House

Gary's final words—"I think you need a place to reflect on your failures"—snapped the tension in the room. AJ didn't wait for the inevitable attack. He grabbed Scarlett's arm and pulled her fiercely toward the front door.

Jade, white-faced and terrified, was frozen near the kitchen. Gary was already standing, reaching under the massive cream sofa for what was clearly a weapon. AJ shoved Scarlett out onto the landing first, pulling the door shut behind them with a violent slam.

"Run!" AJ commanded, his voice tight.

Jade stumbled onto the landing, clutching the neck of her shirt, paralyzed by shock and confusion. AJ didn't waste a second trying to reason with her; he made a brutal, instantaneous calculation: Scarlett's injuries and status required immediate extraction. He shoved Scarlett down the stairwell first, his hand clamped around her arm like a vise.

"I can't just leave her!" Scarlett protested, trying to pull back towards Jade.

"She's frozen! We don't have time!" AJ hissed, wrenching Scarlett forward. "Every second we stay here is a risk to you!"

He pulled Scarlett past the lower floors, ignoring the sound of muffled shouting from above. They raced out of the building, past the skip, and into the maze of back alleys and abandoned buildings that bordered the council estate. He pulled Scarlett deeper into the industrial zone. They moved like ghosts through the abandoned suburbs, their pace frantic, fueled by the imminent pursuit.

AJ finally stopped, shoving her through a rotten, boarded-up door of a decaying terrace house just off the estate boundary. Dust, cold, and the smell of mold hit them instantly.

"Lock it," AJ breathed, his chest heaving. "This is a temporary fallback. No power, no heating. It won't be in their immediate search pattern."

Scarlett leaned against the door, every muscle screaming, her mind a dizzying blur of gunshots, betrayal, and abandonment. Her bruised body was a roadmap of stitches and aches. AJ turned, his eyes dark, mirroring the exhaustion and violent fear that gripped her.

He didn't speak. He slammed her back against the damp, plaster wall. "I almost lost you," he choked out, his voice thick with raw emotion. He grabbed her face, kissing her with a starved ferocity that was shocking and necessary. It was a kiss of terror, relief, and pure survival.

She responded instantly, twisting into him, needing the hard, real anchor of his body against the unreality of the last few hours. The shock of Gary's betrayal and the looming threat—that they were trapped in the heart of the network—ignited a desperate, reckless fire. The muffled sound of shouting from the distant estate was muted by the walls, but present.

AJ silenced all of it. His mouth devoured hers; his hands moved with an urgency that stripped away the last layers of fear, leaving only desire. There was no gentleness, no exploration, only a raw, primal claim driven by the certainty that this might be the last moment they had. The borrowed clothes were ripped off and tossed against the damp floorboards.

The room was cramped, cold, smelling faintly of mold and plaster dust. He lifted her easily, pressing her back against the cold, rough wall. The roughness was terrifyingly real, a confirmation of the violence they were escaping, a direct rebellion against the men who wanted her.

Their intimacy here was chaotic and loud, a furious burst of life against the face of death. She cried out, muffling the sound against his neck, digging her fingers into the taut muscles of his back. Every thrust was a desperate assertion of life, a scream of defiance against Gary, against the lies, against the police who had suspended him. When the storm finally passed, they collapsed onto the dusty, cold floor, tangled together and utterly silent, listening only to the frantic sound of their own hearts.

The Next Step

After a minute of ragged, necessary silence, AJ pushed himself up. He was already the detective again, the survival clock ticking.

"We have to move," he said, pulling her up with him. "We can't stay here. This is only a stopgap."

He retrieved a small duffel bag he'd stashed in the corner. "Quick change," he muttered, tossing her a pair of fresh, dark jogging bottoms and a thick hoodie. He pulled on a clean, dark t-shirt and jeans himself.

They moved like ghosts through the abandoned streets, reaching the vehicle. "We're clear," he stated, pulling out onto a narrow country road.

Chapter 27: The Car Crash

They moved like ghosts through the abandoned suburbs, the cold, stale air biting at their faces. Their brief stop at the boarded-up house had been necessary, but they had consumed precious minutes of their escape window. They finally reached the last service vehicle AJ had access to—a discreet, older-model car, dull and unremarkable—which he had stashed several blocks from the main estate.

AJ worked quickly, throwing the engine over. The worn machine coughed to life, sounding louder than a siren in the quiet urban decay. "We're clear," he stated, his voice a low, steady rumble, pulling out onto a narrow country road that promised a quick route to the motorway. For three tense minutes, the road behind them was empty, lit only by the faint glow of distant streetlights.

Then, Scarlett saw it.

"We have company."

The headlights of a powerful 4x4 were burning relentlessly behind them, not just following, but gaining speed with ruthless intent. It wasn't the tentative tailing of a cautious driver; it was an aggressive, predatory pursuit.

"They didn't find us. They predicted the route," AJ snarled, gripping the wheel so tightly his knuckles were white. He spared a quick glance at the rearview mirror, his eyes narrowing to slits. "Everyone runs for the main line here. They knew exactly where to cut us off. Hold on!"

He slammed the accelerator, the older car groaning in protest, desperately trying to pull away. But the 4x4 was bigger, faster, and driven by lethal intent.

The rear-view mirror filled with chrome and blinding light. The 4x4 slammed hard into AJ's rear quarter panel. A sickening CRUNCH of metal on metal ripped through the quiet night, accompanied by the shriek of tortured tires. The impact spun the service car violently, sending it careening off the road in a chaotic, uncontrolled skid. The world became a dizzying blur of mud, headlights, and shattering glass. The car rolled once, then twice, before slamming to a final, brutal stop in a deep, muddy ditch.

The smell of gasoline and hot oil filled the ruined silence.

"AJ!" she choked out, disoriented and battered, the airbag deflated around her face.

He was slumped against the steering wheel, his breathing ragged. "We need to go," he muttered, his voice thick with pain, already reaching for his door handle.

The passenger door was mangled but, miraculously, still operational. Scarlett shoved it open with a desperate surge of adrenaline, scrambling out into the freezing mud and rain. She hit the ground hard, ignoring the fresh spike of pain in her ribs.

AJ was slower, favoring his left side, but he emerged swiftly. He grabbed her hand, his grasp like a steel cable, pulling her deeper into the thick, dark line of trees that bordered the ditch.

They ran, soaked and terrified, the sound of car doors slamming shut and heavy boots hitting the asphalt echoing behind them. This time, the chase was personal and professional. They were captured, yet again, but this time, they had no safe houses, no police connections, and no friendly walls to hide behind. The protocol was dead; they were simply running for their lives.

Chapter 28: Interception

The sound of the powerful 4x4's engine idling felt deafeningly loud against the quiet sigh of the freezing November rain. Every beat of the idling motor was a clock ticking toward their capture. Scarlett and AJ scrambled through the heavy, sodden undergrowth, the cold mud sucking at their feet.

"We can't outrun them," AJ grunted, the pain from the car crash and his existing injuries visibly slowing him. "They know the terrain better than we do."

"They'll cut the road," Scarlett panted, trying to push past a thicket of brambles. "They're flanking us." She knew, even in her terror, that military precision was guiding their pursuers. Gary wasn't just a dealer; he was a commander.

From their left, a powerful flashlight beam cut brutally through the trees, sweeping the gloom like a searchlight. "Move!" AJ hissed, shoving her forward. Just as the light faded, two more figures emerged from the gloom ahead, heavy, looming shapes that completely blocked their path. Both were bulky, dressed in dark tactical gear, carrying thick wooden batons.

"Drop it, copper," one of the men called out, his voice heavy and flat.

"Arthur," the voice of a third man, slick and chillingly calm, sliced through the air from directly behind them. Gary.

Gary stepped into the faint glow of the distant headlights, holding a massive umbrella, looking incongruously dry and pristine amid the mud and chaos. "My contact gave me a full transcription of your little call to Deedee the moment you ended the transmission. We knew you were compromised for days."

AJ didn't react visibly, but the shock of a mole inside his own specialist unit visibly drained the remaining color from his face. The entire operation—his entire life—had been compromised from within. "She's civilian, Gary. You touch her, and every unit in the country will be on your ass."

Gary smiled, a wide, reptilian grin. "But by morning, you and your clever little lawyer will be in a container bound for the continent. And Michael wants a word about that bullet wound." He closed the distance, his voice turning darkly patronizing.

"You, Arthur, are going straight to the interrogation room. We need to know who else in that unit knows my name." Gary paused, enjoying the agony of his revelation. "As for your little solicitor..." He sighed dramatically, tilting his head. "She's too high-grade to waste. We'll clean her up, keep her looking pretty with a steady supply of product, and put her to work on the circuit."

"She will be passed around my network until she's earning her keep, Arthur. You, however, will be passed around the interrogation room until you're useless."

AJ roared, a sound of pure, unadulterated rage and despair. He shoved Scarlett sideways with a violent force designed to send her sprawling. He then launched himself with desperate, reckless fury at the nearest guard.

But they were prepared. One of the men behind them swung the baton. The second connected savagely with AJ's already bandaged shoulder. AJ went down with a choked cry of agony, his defensive posture instantly shattered.

Scarlett scrambled to her feet, screaming. "Let go!" she shrieked, fueled by terror and adrenaline, knowing exactly what Gary planned for them both.

"Don't worry, sweetheart," the thug who had stayed back growled, yanking her back and slamming her hard against a tree trunk. She felt the impact rattle her teeth.

She watched, helpless, her vision blurring, as the two remaining men dragged AJ's unresponsive body through the mud, his movements limp. Gary tutted softly, a sound of final, chilling victory. Darkness rushed over Scarlett as a thick cloth was pulled roughly over her head, muffling her desperate cries. The last thing she heard, before the absolute blackness swallowed her, was the sickening sound of AJ being dragged away.

Chapter 29: The Witness Box

The transition from the freezing rain of the ditch to the stifling darkness of the transport was violent and utterly disorienting. Scarlett's head throbbed, her ribs screamed with every bump, and the stale chemical smell of the sack over her face made her gag violently. She was lifted, thrown, and jostled, the rough handling amplifying her terror until she felt less like a person and more like a sack of damaged goods.

The noise eventually stopped. The canvas sack was ripped off her head. Scarlett blinked rapidly against the sudden, harsh glare of a single, naked overhead bulb. She was in a concrete room—a makeshift interrogation cell, soundproofed and cold. The air smelled of damp, chlorine, and sweat. She was secured to a steel chair bolted to the floor, her wrists cuffed behind her back, the cold metal biting into her skin and sending familiar jolts of fear through her arms.

Across the room, against the far wall, was AJ. He was in a matching steel chair, but he wasn't upright. His body was slumped, his head lolling to one side, held only by the cuffs securing his hands above his head to a heavy metal rail bolted near the ceiling. He was barely conscious, breathing shallowly, his face a mess of bruises, drying blood, and fresh mud.

The Uncooperative Copper

The steel door hissed open, and Gary strolled into the room, now holding a medical kit instead of an umbrella. He was followed by Michael, the enormous thug AJ had shot, whose expression was a terrifying mix of pain, simmering vengeance, and anticipation. Michael carried the heavy wooden baton, tapping it lightly against his palm.

"Ah, good. Welcome to the theatre, solicitor," Gary said brightly, pulling up a clean plastic stool for himself, positioning it directly opposite Scarlett. "We have an agenda, and your copper boyfriend here is being a bit uncooperative. He seems to value his employment records over your welfare. Perhaps you can inspire him."

Gary snapped his fingers. Michael walked behind AJ, grabbing a fistful of his hair and jerking his head upright, exposing the bruised mess of his face. "Eyes open, Arthur. Time for your next debrief."

AJ moaned, his eyes fluttering open with effort. The moment he saw Scarlett—secured, bruised, and clearly terrified—a primal, guttural noise ripped from his throat. He strained against the elevated cuffs, the metal chains rattling against the rail as he fought, uselessly, against the restraints. "You son of a bitch," AJ choked out, his voice hoarse and broken with fresh fury.

"Language, Arthur," Gary admonished lightly. "Now, before we get to your operational passwords, we need to address the solicitor's health. All this running around is terribly bad for the complexion. And we need her compliant for her new job."

The Conditioning

Gary opened the medical kit. He pulled out a syringe and a small, unlabeled vial of liquid, the sight of which was enough to break Scarlett's composure entirely.

Scarlett screamed, thrashing against her restraints, twisting desperately in the chair. "No! Get away from me! Don't you dare!"

AJ roared, his voice tearing. "Don't you fucking touch her, Gary! I swear to God!" His desperate shouts bounced off the concrete, the sound of a strong man breaking. He thrashed against his elevated cuffs, his body convulsing in pure, frantic horror, watching the controlled violence used on Scarlett.

Gary smiled, ignoring their pleas. "She's quite the looker, isn't she, Arthur? A shame to waste all that beauty on a judge's bench. But don't worry, we're professionals. We keep our girls functioning, earning top dollar. And Michael here is going to ensure she stays firmly put."

Michael grabbed her hair, forcing her head back with agonizing pressure. The sound was immediately muffled as Michael slapped her hard across the face, the force snapping her head sideways and leaving her gasping. He then grabbed the thick baton and brought it down hard across her thigh—a controlled, agonizing strike that caused a flash of white-hot pain and a muffled scream that tasted like blood. AJ screamed again—a raw, broken sound of absolute agony that echoed off the concrete walls.

Gary injected the liquid into Scarlett's arm, holding her down with professional ease. "That's just for the pain, Arthur. And to relax the mind. We need her compliant, earning money. Michael has strict instructions not to damage the product too badly. But the initial conditioning... that's always rough."

Scarlett felt the drug hit her bloodstream—a cold wave followed by a dizzying rush of heat. Her frantic struggles weakened instantly. Her muscles went slack, her mind detached, floating away from the throbbing pain and the suffocating fear. Through the rising haze, she heard AJ's screams—desperate, heartbroken bellows of a man utterly broken by what he was forced to witness. "No! Stop! Don't touch her! I'll tell you everything! Leave her alone!"

Gary smiled, perfectly satisfied. He nodded to Michael, who stepped back, leaving Scarlett slumped, drugged, and weeping silently, her fight gone. "Good, Arthur. Now we can begin. Let's start with the name of the mole who leaked you the raid timing..."

Chapter 30: The Interrogation

The world for Scarlett had dissolved into thick, warm cotton. Her limbs were heavy, useless, and the brutal reality of the concrete room existed only as a muted backdrop to the dizzying, gentle rush in her head. The drug—likely a potent benzodiazepine like Rohypnol, she realized distantly, the legal terms surfacing even through the haze—had done its work. She was slumped in the steel chair, her head resting against the rail of the cuffs, the localized pain in her thigh sharp but manageable—a distant throb beneath the pharmacological veil.

She could see AJ, but only in fragments. He was a terrifying sight: cuffed above his head, body hanging limply save for the frantic strains against the restraints. She was aware of his movement, the guttural sounds, but they were filtered, softened, like noise heard underwater. Gary's voice, however, was agonizingly clear, slicing through the drug's effect like a scalpel.

"You're a hero, Arthur," Gary cooed, pacing slowly, his leather shoes clicking on the concrete. "You chose the girl over the job. Noble. Very noble. But heroism is expensive. It costs you your career, your freedom, and, soon, your mind."

AJ stayed silent, his eyes locked on Scarlett. His focus was entirely on ensuring she was still breathing, still present, using the last of his will to project protection across the room.

The Operational Code

Gary produced a small, laminated photo—an older picture of AJ in uniform, standing beside a serious, dark-haired woman in a clean police uniform. "This is your boss, isn't it? Detective Inspector Deedee Hayes? Now, I just need to know how she reports her losses to the command structure. Give me the code or the procedure. You have ten seconds."

AJ spat weakly, the blood-flecked saliva hitting Gary's expensive coat. It was a final, desperate act of defiance.

"Disappointing. Michael, introduce yourself to the solicitor. We need to test the merchandise."

Michael walked over to Scarlett, his heavy steps reverberating through the floor, a sound that bypassed the drug haze entirely. He ran his calloused hand down her cheek. "Stunning, isn't she? I'm going to enjoy this," he snarled, the threat immediate and visceral. He took hold of her handcuffs and wrenched the entire chair over. Scarlett thudded down onto the concrete floor in an awkward heap, helpless and tangled in the restraints.

Michael dragged her legs straight and produced a flick knife. The glint of the steel was the final, defining image of the torture. With one quick snarl of the knife, he sliced the drawstring holding her tracksuit bottoms closed, the fabric yielding easily.

AJ roared, straining against the cuffs, his body convulsing in pure, frantic horror, witnessing the final violation of his protective boundary. His screams were those of a man breaking irrevocably. "NO! STOP! OKAY! For fuck sake, OKAY! I'll tell you! I'll tell you everything!"

Fallow Ground

Gary smiled, perfectly satisfied, waving Michael back. "The operational code name for reporting agent failure, Arthur. Give it to me now."

AJ's body hung limp from the rail, his resistance shattered. His voice was a ragged, barely audible whisper, thick with defeat and self-loathing. "It's... it's 'Fallow Ground'," he choked out. "The full debrief procedure is Fallow Ground."

Gary smiled, a slow, deep expression of absolute triumph. "Fallow Ground. Excellent. You see, Arthur? You just had to be inspired. Now we know exactly when Deedee will be reporting your loss, and how. You've given us the entire schedule."

"Right, Arthur," Gary announced, pulling his stool away. "Now that we have the counter-intel sorted, we move to Stage Two. You've been very naughty, resisting arrest. We need to teach you discipline." He nodded to Michael. "Michael, start with the face. And make sure our little solicitor here can hear everything clearly."

The thick ropes were produced, replacing the need for Michael's physical attendance. Scarlett tried to twist her head, tried to scream, but the Rophynol held her captive, a screaming prisoner in her own heavy, useless body. The last thing she registered, before the sound of the first impact and AJ's sharp, choked cry of renewed pain, was the knowledge that her presence hadn't just compromised him—it had utterly destroyed him.

Chapter 30: The Interrogation

The world for Scarlett had dissolved into thick, warm cotton. Her limbs were heavy, useless, and the brutal reality of the concrete room existed only as a muted backdrop to the dizzying, gentle rush in her head. The drug—likely a potent benzodiazepine like Rohypnol, she realized distantly, the legal terms surfacing even through the haze—had done its work. She was slumped in the steel chair, her head resting against the rail of the cuffs, the localized pain in her thigh sharp but manageable—a distant throb beneath the pharmacological veil.

She could see AJ, but only in fragments. He was a terrifying sight: cuffed above his head, body hanging limply save for the frantic strains against the restraints. She was aware of his movement, the guttural sounds, but they were filtered, softened, like noise heard underwater. Gary's voice, however, was agonizingly clear, slicing through the drug's effect like a scalpel.

"You're a hero, Arthur," Gary cooed, pacing slowly, his leather shoes clicking on the concrete. "You chose the girl over the job. Noble. Very noble. But heroism is expensive. It costs you your career, your freedom, and, soon, your mind."

AJ stayed silent, his eyes locked on Scarlett. His focus was entirely on ensuring she was still breathing, still present, using the last of his will to project protection across the room.

The Operational Code

Gary produced a small, laminated photo—an older picture of AJ in uniform, standing beside a serious, dark-haired woman in a clean police uniform. "This is your boss, isn't it? Detective Inspector Deedee Hayes? Now, I just need to know how she reports her losses to the command structure. Give me the code or the procedure. You have ten seconds."

AJ spat weakly, the blood-flecked saliva hitting Gary's expensive coat. It was a final, desperate act of defiance.

"Disappointing. Michael, introduce yourself to the solicitor. We need to test the merchandise."

Michael walked over to Scarlett, his heavy steps reverberating through the floor, a sound that bypassed the drug haze entirely. He ran his calloused hand down her cheek. "Stunning, isn't she? I'm going to enjoy this," he snarled, the threat immediate and visceral. He took hold of her handcuffs and wrenched the entire chair over. Scarlett thudded down onto the concrete floor in an awkward heap, helpless and tangled in the restraints.

Michael dragged her legs straight and produced a flick knife. The glint of the steel was the final, defining image of the torture. With one quick snarl of the knife, he sliced the drawstring holding her tracksuit bottoms closed, the fabric yielding easily.

AJ roared, straining against the cuffs, his body convulsing in pure, frantic horror, witnessing the final violation of his protective boundary. His screams were those of a man breaking irrevocably. "NO! STOP! OKAY! For fuck sake, OKAY! I'll tell you! I'll tell you everything!"

Fallow Ground

Gary smiled, perfectly satisfied, waving Michael back. "The operational code name for reporting agent failure, Arthur. Give it to me now."

AJ's body hung limp from the rail, his resistance shattered. His voice was a ragged, barely audible whisper, thick with defeat and self-loathing. "It's... it's 'Fallow Ground'," he choked out. "The full debrief procedure is Fallow Ground."

Gary smiled, a slow, deep expression of absolute triumph. "Fallow Ground. Excellent. You see, Arthur? You just had to be inspired. Now we know exactly when Deedee will be reporting your loss, and how. You've given us the entire schedule."

"Right, Arthur," Gary announced, pulling his stool away. "Now that we have the counter-intel sorted, we move to Stage Two. You've been very naughty, resisting arrest. We need to teach you discipline." He nodded to Michael. "Michael, start with the face. And make sure our little solicitor here can hear everything clearly."

The thick ropes were produced, replacing the need for Michael's physical attendance. Scarlett tried to twist her head, tried to scream, but the Rophynol held her captive, a screaming prisoner in her own heavy, useless body. The last thing she registered, before the sound of the first impact and AJ's sharp, choked cry of renewed pain, was the knowledge that her presence hadn't just compromised him—it had utterly destroyed him.

Chapter 31: Fallow Lies

The pain was not distant for AJ; it was absolute. Each strike from the heavy wooden baton was a fresh, white-hot explosion against his back and ribs, fueling a cold, desperate rage. Worse than the physical fire, however, was the sound of Scarlett's muted, drug-induced whimpering—the evidence of his failure echoing in the confines of the concrete room. Gary had left over an hour ago, satisfied with AJ's 'confession' of "Fallow Ground."

Michael, the guard, stood gloating, tapping the baton against his scarred palm. He stopped when AJ spoke, his voice ragged but suddenly clear.

"Fallow Ground doesn't exist, you know," AJ gasped out, forcing the words through bruised lungs. He lifted his head, a grim, defiant glint in his eyes. "It's a field manual I burned ten years ago. It's utter rubbish. You wasted your time. You gave Gary rubbish."

Michael roared in frustrated rage, the realization that he'd been fooled and that the last hour of brutal torture had been meaningless hitting him instantly. He slammed the baton against the wall.

"I know I bought her six hours," AJ whispered, his gaze flicking to Scarlett. The Rohypnol was wearing off just enough to let her feel the terrible, damp chill of the concrete. He began to move, testing the heavy steel cuffs securing his hands above his head. The chair, though bolted to the concrete floor, had been repeatedly stressed during his earlier thrashing. With a sudden, tearing SCREEECH, one of the steel plates ripped free from the concrete anchor.

Michael rushed forward, swinging the baton in a wide, vicious arc. AJ slammed the freed steel chair down hard across Michael's skull, the heavy metal connecting with a dull thud. Michael dropped instantly like a sack of stones.

The noise of the impact alerted the guard posted outside the cell door. A warning shot tore a chunk of plaster from the concrete wall near AJ's head, fired from the hallway. Before the guard could properly aim, AJ launched himself towards the door, catching the guard's wrist, twisting the gun away, the momentum sending the weapon skittering across the floor and out of reach.

The Solicitor's Protocol

AJ rushed to Scarlett, his movements stiff but driven. He grabbed the fallen guard's keys and worked furiously at the heavy, cold restraints. The metal clicked free. "We have to move! Now!" he muttered, scanning the hallway outside the cell door.

Scarlett swayed, fighting the nausea and forcing her mind through the fog. She wasn't a fighter in the traditional sense, but she was a solicitor—she was trained to analyze structure, weak points, and procedure. She grabbed the guard's abandoned pistol, its weight cold and surprising in her hand.

"Door's heavy," she slurred, her voice thick and weak, but her mind cutting through the haze. "Steel door.

Three hinges. We need to hit the bottom hinge first to break the load-bearing stress."

AJ looked at the bruised, drugged woman in front of him, her finger already resting lightly on the trigger, analyzing structural weak points and giving him tactical advice. It was the last, most surreal moment of the night. "Arthur—the rope," she reminded him, indicating the heavy hemp ropes Gary's men had brought in for the second stage of his torture.

He scooped her up, tucking her against his less-damaged shoulder, ignoring the searing pain. He wrapped the heavy rope around his shoulder and the door handle for extra leverage. He used his last reserve of strength to kick the bottom hinge of the steel door twice, then the lock, sending the door flying open with a deafening crash that echoed through the complex. They stumbled out of the cell and into the dark, echoing complex, escaping into the unknown.

Chapter 32: The Drumming Heart

The complex was a disorienting labyrinth of concrete corridors and humming machinery, smelling strongly of ethanol and stale chemicals. Every surface was cold, metallic, and unforgiving. The distant rhythmic thump of heavy machinery—the operational 'bassline' that Gary had referred to—vibrated through the soles of Scarlett's feet, guiding them deeper into the facility.

"Processing plant," AJ muttered, leaning heavily on the wall for support. The sheer sound density made it impossible to hear anything localized. "The noise masks everything else. They can run heavy equipment and scream all they want; no one outside will hear it."

They reached a junction where the corridor split into two identical, forbidding paths. AJ pressed his ear to the cold steel door on the left. "Voices," he whispered, pushing off the wall. "Too many. And too close."

Scarlett closed her eyes, fighting the narcotic fog that still muffled her thoughts. Her solicitor's mind, however, was stubbornly trying to gain control. "We need to know the layout. Find the schematics. Server room, maybe?"

AJ dismissed this with a sharp shake of his head. "Too deep. That's where they store the intel. We don't have time. We find the exit, the service tunnel, anything that leads outside."

She used the keys they had taken from Michael to unlock the heavy steel shackle that remained dangling from his free wrist. She pressed the keys into his palm. "No time for the rope trick again."

"You're going to hold the gun," AJ instructed, his voice low and firm. He took the retrieved pistol from the floor. "I need my hands free." He pressed the cold metal weapon into her grip. "My job now is navigation and leverage." He checked the chamber, then tucked the weapon back into her waistband.

The steel door on the right opened suddenly. Two uniformed guards stepped into the hall, carrying plastic crates. AJ slammed his bruised body and Scarlett's against the wall just as the guards passed, their heavy boots thudding past their hiding spot. The men didn't even glance their way, lost in the facility's ambient noise.

They continued until they reached a massive, double-hinged steel door with a prominent red 'Danger: High Voltage' warning sign bolted to its surface.

"The heart," AJ breathed, his eyes assessing the fortification. "The operational centre. This is where Gary would be running things, coordinating the clean-up."

"We stick together," she insisted, leaning into him, her gaze meeting his. The Rohypnol haze was fading enough to allow the protective instinct to override the fear. "We move as one unit."

AJ nodded, a flicker of appreciation for her resilience crossing his face. "Fine. You watch my six. If you see movement, you shout, lawyer." He wedged the barrel of the gun—the very weapon he had used to save her life—into the hinge of the double doors, using it as a lever to pry the heavy steel open.

The room beyond was vast, huge, lit only by flashing red and green warning lights that cast distorted shadows across stacks of crates and heavy machinery. It was a fortified staging area, smelling intensely of processed chemicals and fuel.

Standing by the communication bank, perfectly positioned and waiting, was Gary.

"Arthur," Gary drawled, his voice amplified slightly by the acoustics of the huge room. He was holding a secured radio set, not a soldering iron, confirming his role as commander. "I knew you were too predictable to run. I expected you back." He looked past AJ to

Scarlett, his grin chilling. "Didn't think you'd bring the product, though."

He pointed with a manicured hand at a far corner where a steel ladder led up to a hatch high in the ceiling. "That's the only way out, Arthur. The roof. And with your shoulder, and her condition, you're not going to make it."

Chapter 33: The Hatch

"You see that? That's the only way out, and you're not going to make it." Gary's voice was triumphant, resonating through the large, echoing staging area. The steel ladder leading fifty feet up to the roof hatch was impossibly far away, and two armed guards were already closing the distance on either side of the chemical mixer.

"Scarlett, the whiteboard," AJ yelled, his eyes darting desperately around the room for a viable target that wasn't Gary. "Logistics! See what you can ruin!"

AJ didn't wait for her confirmation. He fired the pistol—the guard's own weapon—with a grunt, aiming with his good hand. The shot was aimed high, striking the main overhead light fixture near the center of the room. The bulb exploded, and the vast area plunged into a near-total, blinding darkness, punctuated only by the strobing red and green emergency lights.

Two guards instantly materialized from the resulting shadows, their heavy silhouettes moving toward the sound of the blast. AJ shoved the gun back into Scarlett's hand. "Cover me! Aim for the mixers! The big churning ones! Blind them!"

Scarlett, despite swaying on her feet and fighting the persistent narcotic fog, found a deadly, cold clarity. She aimed the heavy pistol at the nearest large, churning industrial mixer, a chemical heart of the operation. The bullet struck the metal casing with a deafening *CLANG*, and the mixer shrieked, instantly coughing a massive cloud of white, acrid chemical powder into the air. The substance was toxic, blinding, and instantly disorienting.

"The ladder, Arthur!" Scarlett yelled, hacking violently into the chemical smoke, the acrid dust burning her eyes and lungs. Her diversion was perfect. She fired a second shot towards a cluster of communication equipment, the noise forcing the guards to duck further into the smoke.

The Climb and the Collapse

AJ scrambled toward the ladder, his bad shoulder protesting with every agonizing vertical pull, but driven by pure necessity. The smoke was now thick enough to conceal them completely, transforming the staging area into a choking, invisible hell for the guards.

"Scarlett! They're past the mixer! They'll be on the ladder!" AJ hissed, his voice tight with pain, but his mind sharp with tactical awareness. Gary's enraged voice cut through the air, muffled by the smoke, as he furiously directed his men below.

AJ reached the hatch, a heavy steel lid secured by a massive, industrial lock. He fumbled with the complex mechanism, his fingers thick with grime and blood, muttering curses under his breath as the cold metal resisted. Finally, with a loud, metallic *CLICK*, the lock yielded. A glorious rush of cold, clean night air poured into the stifling, chemical-laced room below, clearing the smoke directly around the ladder base.

Time was running out. AJ secured one end of the hemp rope—the very rope intended for his torture—around the base of the ladder, ensuring it was taut and secure against the wall. "You go first," he commanded, his voice sharp and professional, the tone of command leaving no room for debate. "I'll follow and break the ladder."

Scarlett didn't argue. Despite her wooziness, she knew this was the one chance. The smoke was already thinning. She scrambled up through the opening, pulling her heavy, aching body free of the staging area and onto the flat, cold surface of the roof.

AJ followed immediately, ignoring the searing, explosive pain in his shoulder as he hauled himself through the opening. His weight slammed down onto the weakened ladder one last time, driving his heel against the supporting bolts. The structure groaned and tore away from the wall where it had been stressed by the stress of his frantic climb. The last thing Scarlett heard was the metallic screech of the ladder tumbling down onto the concrete floor of the staging area, followed instantly by Gary's enraged, muffled roar of total defeat. They were sealed in the dark, narrow tunnel, the ultimate escape route now destroyed behind them. They had bought themselves minutes, and nothing more.

Chapter 34: The Dark Slide

The ventilation shaft was a nightmare of cold, greasy metal and suffocating blackness. The air was thick with dust and the lingering scent of chemicals from the staging area. The sheer relief of sealing the hatch was immediately replaced by the acute, terrifying reality of their confinement.

Scarlett slid blindly down the rope AJ had secured, the friction burning her tracksuit-covered palms. The remaining Rohypnol in her system made her coordination dangerously slow and her movements clumsy. Below her, the shaft dropped at a steep, unforgiving angle.

"Just keep your feet against the wall," AJ choked out from above, his voice tight with pain and strain. "Use the pressure points. Don't slip."

They were safe from immediate pursuit, but trapped within the ventilation system, their only escape route was now linear. The structural integrity of the duct was their only hope.

She reached a sudden, sharp bend where the main shaft narrowed significantly. She was forced to abandon the rope and begin crawling. AJ followed, dropping heavily beside her, the sound of his armored heel plates scraping metal echoing loudly.

"Follow the airflow," AJ whispered, his breath hot against her ear. "The intake leads outside, or to a major exhaust stack. We pray for outside."

She had to push blindly, desperately, backward with her heels and elbows, the effort straining her already damaged ribs. The rhythmic, grinding sound of a power tool pursued them relentlessly through the metal tube. It was Gary's men, trying to breach the system.

The tunnel eventually opened into a large, cold, horizontal metal tube—the main duct. The space here was wider, and the air moved faster, smelling sharply of diesel and fresh asphalt. "Smell the fuel," AJ murmured, his voice gaining clarity. "We're above the loading bay or the vehicle prep area. Closer to the perimeter."

The Plasma Threat

Suddenly, the cold air was replaced by an intense, searing heat that rushed over them, quickly followed by the stench of burning paint and superheated metal.

"Fire!" Scarlett gasped, shoving herself against the floor of the duct.

"No, torch!" AJ corrected, his voice snapping with immediate operational assessment. "Welding torch! He didn't flood the system; he's cutting a panel! He knows we're in the main duct!"

The piercing whine of a plasma cutter shrieked through the metal, deafening them. The heat intensified, and a blinding, brilliant sliver of white-hot light appeared directly ahead, slicing through the darkness of the duct. Gary hadn't resorted to climbing; he was simply cutting the duct open where it was most accessible.

AJ scrambled backward instantly, his survival instincts overriding the crippling pain in his shoulder. He shoved Scarlett behind him with surprising force. "Reverse! Now! Go back! Go back! He's cutting the line! We have to find an exhaust vent!"

The sudden, chaotic reversal forced Scarlett into a blind, terrifying crawl back into the dark, narrow passage they had just left. The sound of the plasma cutter shrieked, growing closer, transforming their metal escape route into a steel furnace.

Chapter 35: Fugitives in the Peak

The plasma cutter's shriek chased them backward through the cold, greasy duct. AJ was forced to move on pure, primal instinct, pulling Scarlett behind him until they reached the wider crawlspace where they'd started the descent. The air was thick and metallic, stinging their lungs.

"Wait! The cutter stopped," Scarlett whispered, hacking as she tried to clear the toxic residue from her throat. The lingering Rophynol was now mixing with the noxious fumes, leaving her desperately sick and terrified.

"He's not cutting the exit; he's cutting the access panel closest to us," AJ grated out, retrieving the pistol from his waistband and checking the remaining rounds. "He knows this network. He wants to see us squirm. We have seconds before he drops the panel and finds us."

With a final, desperate surge of his good leg, AJ kicked violently at the heavily-stressed concrete junction beneath the crawlspace. The rotten mortar, weakened by the facility's vibrations, finally gave way. The panel collapsed, sending them both tumbling ten feet down into a dark, muddy drainage pit. The impact jarred Scarlett's ribs and stitched wound, but the air here was cleaner, smelling of wet earth and decay—a blessed relief from the chemical smoke.

AJ scrambled up, adrenaline masking the fire in his broken shoulder, and dragged Scarlett over the rim of the pit. They were in a wooded copse bordering a large, brightly lit industrial complex—Gary's domain.

They ran, fueled by desperation, using the deep shadows of the trees for cover. AJ managed to hotwire an unmarked white transit van in less than a minute, his military training overriding the fatigue and the crippling pain. They drove hard and fast, sticking to back roads and avoiding motorways, fueled by the combined remaining emergency cash they had salvaged from AJ's brief return home. Their destination: the anonymity of the Peak District hills.

The Emergency Call

It was nearly dawn when AJ pulled the van into a quiet layby near a dilapidated pub. The first gray light of morning was breaking, and they were running on fumes. Scarlett, recognizing the urgent need to confirm the intel, saw what they needed: a battered, old payphone booth standing near the pub's entrance, a relic of a bygone era, and completely untraceable.

"The police lines are compromised," AJ said, his voice flat, staring at the phone booth with grim determination. "But Deedee has an emergency personal scramble number. It's high risk, but we have to confirm Drayton."

Scarlett nodded, handing him the coins she'd found in the van's glove box. "Give her the location of the plant. Tell her everything. Don't hide the mole—tell her Gary has a direct line to the unit."

AJ entered the booth. The conversation was short, brutal, and entirely one-sided. AJ emerged moments later, his face etched with bone-deep despair and utter exhaustion.

"She confirmed Drayton," he rasped, the mole's name a bitter taste on his tongue. "The analyst was running interference for months. They've launched a full, silent internal sweep. She used the intelligence to hit the plant, but... The plant was a decoy. They cleared out the high-value product hours before we arrived. Your intel bought us nothing but clean concrete, Scarlett."

Predictive Containment

He leaned heavily against the van, the cold metal reflecting the rising sun. "It's worse, Scarlett. Gary's reach isn't just the unit. Half the local police force—patrols, narcotics, even some lower court officials—are on Gary's payroll. They keep the raves running, redirecting raids and suppressing witnesses.

We're wanted for the murder of Michael and the other guard."

Scarlett stared at him, the magnitude of the disaster hitting her like a physical blow. "The news is running our faces right now. The story is 'Disgraced Ex-Military Officer and his Accomplice Lawyer Murder Two for Drug Money.' They're painting us as junkies who went rogue. They've already christened us the Bonnie and Clyde of the Peaks."

"They know we're heading there," AJ stated, looking at the rugged, dark skyline of the distant hills. "Not because they tracked the van, but because it's the most logical move for a target like me."

"But why the Peak District?" Scarlett asked, her voice cracking with exhaustion. "We don't know the Peak District."

"It's containment," AJ explained, pushing off the van. "Gary uses predictive modeling based on military behavior. Where does a trained, broken operative, who knows he needs isolation but is close to resources, go? The Peaks. It's the nearest, largest, most complex area for tactical evasion. We ditch this van a mile in, find an old bothy or a secluded quarry. We're running on empty, Scarlett. And our only assets are the clothes on our backs and the truth nobody believes."

Chapter 36: The Bothy and the Divide

The white transit van bounced violently across the moorland track, its aging suspension screaming in protest against the harsh, desolate terrain of the Peak District. They drove until the vehicle was utterly spent, its fuel gauge resting on zero. This was the final, non-negotiable step of their operational plan.

"This is it," he announced, cutting the engine. The resulting silence was immense, heavy, broken only by the sound of the wind whipping across the high peaks and the faint metallic ticking of the cooling engine. He grabbed the last usable item: the stolen pistol, securing it carefully in the waistband of his tracksuit bottoms.

Scarlett, fighting the remaining dregs of the Rophynol and the crushing fatigue, nodded her understanding. They abandoned the van, its bulky white presence a temporary, glaring marker of their path. The ascent was brutal. AJ, relying heavily on his good leg and his core strength to compensate for his useless shoulder, moved with grim, methodical determination, pulling them away from the track and into the immediate shelter of the rocks. The landscape was their new adversary and their only friend.

The Bothy and the Damage

They found shelter three hours later: a small, isolated stone bothy nestled deep within a narrow, rocky coombe. The rough, thick walls provided immediate sanctuary. Inside, it was blessedly dry, if freezing, offering the first temporary reprieve from the bitter wind and the eyes of the local force. AJ, despite his exhaustion, immediately barricaded the small, single window with loose stones, sealing their refuge. He then slumped onto the dirt floor, finally letting the pain win. The exhaustion hit him like a physical illness. He pulled the grey hoodie over his head and, with careful, deliberate movements, examined the damage. His shoulder was swollen to the size of a fist, a gruesome mix of purple and green beneath the dry, cracked skin.

"I need to look at that," Scarlett stated, moving to him. She carefully peeled the makeshift bandages away, her face tightening at the sight of the internal bleeding. Her legal mind instantly reverted to triage mode, prioritizing immediate needs.

"No time," AJ whispered, pushing her hand away gently, his eyes scanning the gaps in the stone wall. "We need to focus on our reality. Gary thinks he has the operational code, 'Fallow Ground.' But the threat is internal. Deedee's unit is compromised, and the local police are working for him. That's our enemy."

Scarlett took his hand firmly, pulling his focus back to the present. "He doesn't have the codes, Arthur. He only has the procedure name. And he doesn't know about the mole in his own network, which is the internal sweep Deedee is running. He's operating blind to that internal threat."

"Jade," AJ cut in, his eyes widening slightly with realization. "She's the collateral, Scarlett. Gary will use her to flush us out."

"He already left her exposed and traumatized," Scarlett argued, the thought of her friend's terror fueling her own resolve. "But she knows too much now. The shock of finding out Gary is a network commander, the realization of his betrayal—that won't just make her collapse. It'll make her angry. And Jade, when angry, is reckless. We need to find a way to warn her, or she'll destroy herself trying to expose him. We need to get a message to her, through a channel Gary won't anticipate."

The Fugitive's Rest

AJ pulled her close, his good arm wrapping around her waist, pulling her into the necessary warmth of his body. "We're done talking, lawyer. We're done planning. We're going to use this isolation. We rest. Then we figure out how to get to Jade without the entirety of local law enforcement finding us."

The gravity of their situation settled heavily between them. They were utterly reliant on each other: AJ provided the tactical knowledge and the physical shield, while Scarlett provided the legal structure and the unpredictable civilian perspective.

The national news was already running their names, detailing the murder of two 'innocent' men, ensuring that every local resident and police officer was looking for the 'Bonnie and Clyde of the Peaks.' They were wanted in their own country, their identities broadcast as cold-blooded killers, and her only ally was the broken man holding her tight in the freezing, absolute silence of the moor.

Chapter 37: The Bothy's Silence

The bothy offered thin, desperate refuge. Its single room, built of rough, damp stone, did nothing to hold the bitter morning cold, but it provided absolute visual isolation. The space was utterly silent, save for the abrasive whisper of the wind scraping against the thick walls and the shallow, painful breathing of its two inhabitants. Scarlett used the fading daylight filtering through the gaps in the window stones to assess their damage.

AJ was slumped in the darkest corner, his posture broken, finally allowing his body to rest after the adrenaline dump. He was an officer of precise, controlled habit, and seeing him in such a state of physical and emotional ruin was more terrifying than any threat. His left shoulder was visibly purple, grossly distorted, and clearly dislocated. He was in profound, quiet pain, his face gray beneath the dirt and bruises.

"I need to put heat on that," Scarlett muttered, the medical urgency overriding the strategic. She rummaged through the small backpack they'd grabbed—a few sterile dressings, emergency energy bars, a detailed map of the Peaks, and a roll of black tactical tape. There were, critically, no painkillers.

"Arthur, the shoulder," she insisted, crawling toward him.

"No. Don't touch it," he managed, his voice a low, pained grate. "I can't risk you setting it wrong. We don't have enough leverage or strength to do it properly, and it'll just break again if we move. It's stable for now."

She accepted the limitation with a sharp intake of breath. Instead, she found a small, half-used tube of deep heat rub—a small miracle salvaged from the abandoned van. She gently massaged the cream around the swollen joint, avoiding direct pressure on the joint itself, working heat into the surrounding, shredded muscles. AJ groaned, biting down hard on his knuckles to muffle the sound, the effort of quiet endurance straining every muscle in his neck and jaw.

The Tactical Window

"The lie won us time," he finally whispered, the effort of speech drawing breath sharp with pain. He was referencing the "Fallow Ground" code he'd fed to Gary. "It means they'll pursue the internal threat, Drayton, which buys us a window before they realize the intelligence is fake. We gave Gary the right level of believable, high-stakes intel to consume his resources internally. But we are counting on a complex internal police sweep."

"And Gary?"

"Gary is currently consolidating. He has the operational name. He thinks he won the trade-off. But he'll predict that if we survived, we'll aim for the most isolated point. This bothy, this entire high-ground area, is effectively his trap. We have to use the terrain and move tonight. We can't stay past nightfall." He paused, his breathing shallow. "We have hours, maybe less, before Deedee starts putting together the pieces and realizes our extraction plan failed. We are running on borrowed time from two opposing forces."

He pulled a small, worn piece of paper from his tracksuit pocket—a tiny, faded picture of the two children, his niece and nephew. He held it tightly, smoothing the creases. "They're safe," he murmured, his voice softening slightly. "They're miles away. But Gary knows their location. I can't risk anything that brings attention back to them, even inadvertently, and that means zero communication until we're fully clear."

Financial Strategy and Rest

Scarlett's legal mind immediately engaged with the logistics. "We need to weaponize our anonymity. We need to become unfindable, not just by Gary's thugs, but by every uniformed officer on his payroll."

"We move by night, we stay hidden by day. We are the ghost operation now," AJ stated, his eyes dark with the strategy of evasion. "The goal is to get to a point where we can hit his finances, not his thugs. We need to freeze his assets, cripple his logistics—that's the only language a commander understands."

"And our legal status gives us leverage," Scarlett argued, her voice gaining strength. "If we can provide irrefutable evidence of Drayton and Gary's network—evidence outside the compromised Met unit—we become valuable witnesses, not wanted fugitives."

AJ nodded, a flicker of appreciation for her resilience crossing his face. "We are counting on the integrity of the system we both know is broken. We have to make ourselves too expensive to kill."

Scarlett nodded, crawling closer. She found the blanket from the bag and draped it over his shivering body. "Rest, Arthur. Just rest. I'll watch the door." She shifted, placing her hand near the cold steel of the pistol he had tucked away. "Your only job is to heal enough to stand up straight. We will move when it is safe. We will find Jade. We will get your life back." She settled beside him, holding the warmth of his body against hers, listening to the high, lonely sound of the wind and the absolute silence of the moorland. Their silence was the only security they possessed.

The bothy smelled of peat, damp stone, sweat, and despair. The air was cold, stinging their lungs. Scarlett woke abruptly, shivering uncontrollably, the rough wool of the blanket offering minimal warmth. AJ was already awake beside her, his breathing shallow and uneven, the sound a tight rasp in the profound darkness.

"Shoulder's locked up," he muttered, his voice strained and quiet. "It's seizing. I need you to tape it."

Scarlett didn't argue. She used the faint, metallic glow from the discarded pistol to locate the roll of black tactical tape in the backpack. She worked awkwardly, the cold stiffening her own bruised fingers, immobilizing his useless left arm tightly against his torso, creating a painful but essential sling. The process was silent save for AJ's sharp, involuntary intakes of breath.

"What's the plan?" she asked once the job was done, needing to impose order on the chaos inside her head.

"North Face," he muttered, using the military term for the coldest, most exposed, and often least-trafficked side of the mountain. "We move onto the high ground. Find a ridge that overlooks the main valleys. They'll search the roads first, they're predictable. We use the height for surveillance, watching the patrol patterns."

His voice grew firmer, reverting to the clipped, tactical rhythm she recognized from the raid. "No stopovers. Every minute we wait is a minute Gary's crew or a crooked uniform gets closer. We move slow, we move silent. We are a ghost operation now, Scarlett. We don't exist."

Assets and Liabilities

Scarlett leaned back against the stone wall, fighting the gnawing fatigue and the reality of their situation by imposing her own structure. She took a mental inventory of their assets:

- Exhibit A: One stolen 9mm pistol (unknown ammo count, unknown provenance).
- Exhibit B: £14.30 in coins and crumpled notes—their entire combined liquidity.
- Exhibit C: One dislocated shoulder (AJ).
- Exhibit D: One Barrister-in-training (Scarlett), wanted for murder.

"The only leverage we have is Jade. And Gary's bank accounts," she stated, listing the non-physical assets.

"Exactly. His finances are the key. He's running an entire ecosystem—moving bulk product, managing logistics, paying off half the city police, and buying his niece a new sofa. He has a complex financial structure," Scarlett mused, the lawyer in her finally finding a solvable puzzle. "We have to find an untraceable terminal—a dark web café or an unmonitored library computer—and start digging into his shell companies. If we can freeze or disrupt his cash flow, we can buy ourselves a window to get proper leverage."

"That requires risk," AJ acknowledged, pulling himself up, using the tactical tape as a lever. "We'll need to break cover, get a signal, and risk contact. And the first signal we send—will be to check on Jonesy."

"Jonesy?" Scarlett frowned, her voice breaking. "Arthur, we're talking about taking down a crime syndicate, and you're talking about the cat? They'd never waste time on him. What if he's still locked in your house, starving?"

AJ met her gaze, his dark eyes intense and steady, but holding a hint of the vulnerability she rarely saw. "I know, Scarlett. He's your family, and he's the only thing clean left in this mess. We need to know he's safe before we do anything else." He squeezed her hand. "And it's tactical. I told Deedee to secure him. If she followed that small, non-operational order, it proves she's loyal enough to receive the big intel. The cat is our test case for the entire Metropolitan Police, Scarlett." It was a deeply personal, rationalized line he was drawing, validating her emotional need through tactical logic.

He picked up the stolen pistol, testing its weight. "Let's walk, lawyer. We have a long night ahead, and we start by getting to that ridge."

Chapter 39: The High Ridge

The ascent onto the high ridge was agonizingly slow, conducted in the biting cold and the gray half-light of the moorland morning. AJ's left arm was plastered tightly against his chest by the black tactical tape, immobilizing his shoulder and making him look permanently half-drawn. Every uneven step was a conscious calculation against the searing pain. Scarlett moved ahead, her smaller frame navigating the treacherous, slippery terrain with more agility. She kept her focus outward, treating the hike like a forced reconnaissance mission.

"We need a name for Gary's financial anchor," Scarlett murmured, keeping her voice low against the wind. Her mind was already three steps ahead, back in the courtroom. "I know the legal structures—we need their Companies House registration details, Arthur. That's Exhibit A."

AJ dropped instantly behind a shelf of exposed rock, pausing to take a rasping, painful breath, scanning the valleys below. "We can't rest. If Deedee acted on the Fallow Ground intel, Gary knows his operational information is compromised. He'll shift his assets, he'll disappear the mole—Drayton—and he'll deploy his local police assets to seal the Peaks."

He pushed himself up, leaning heavily on a walking stick he'd fashioned from a fallen branch. His eyes, though ringed with exhaustion, were burning with a desperate clarity. "The real assets are already liquid or disguised. The financial front will be his main weakness if we hit it quickly."

The Tactical Decision

"We need to risk the radio," AJ decided, the gravity of the statement immense. Breaking silence on a compromised network was the most dangerous thing they could do. "There's a high point nearby—Kinder Scout. It's too exposed, too visible, but it's the only place we'll get enough signal strength to break out of the immediate local network and reach Deedee's secondary scramble number again."

Scarlett consulted the map, her finger tracing the contours in the low light. "It's three hours away at your current speed, minimum. We risk exposure to every hiking group and farmer who decides to walk the summit, and we risk the signal being intercepted by Gary's radio assets."

"It's the best bad option," AJ countered, the phrase flat and emotionless. "We have to know if Jonesy is safe. That is the first condition."

Scarlett knew the sequence was non-negotiable. "If she didn't protect the cat, she won't protect the intel, and we pivot," she summarized. The logic was painful but sound: the highest-stakes test of loyalty rested on the fate of one ginger cat. "If he is safe, we tell her the financial front—that he must have used a central clearing agency or a high-end shell corporation to manage the bulk payments."

"Exactly. That gives Deedee's uncompromised team a target and buys us more time," AJ confirmed.

Legal Threats and Finality

"Fine. We move when the moon sets," Scarlett agreed, tucking the map back into the bag. The time felt arbitrary, but it gave them a goal. "But if a traffic cop sees us, I'm using my legal rights. I'm going to demand a solicitor and lodge a formal complaint against the police force of three counties. I will tie up every asset they commit to our pursuit with so much paperwork they can't move."

AJ actually managed a faint, bloody smile, a brief, startling flash of the man she had met at the rave. "You use your words, lawyer. You cause a magnificent, bureaucratic headache."

He tapped the pistol secured at his waist. "I'll use the gun to ensure you survive long enough to file the first subpoena." The statement wasn't a threat; it was a promise of brutal protection.

With the plan set—a dangerous climb, a high-risk radio call, and the fate of their entire resistance resting on the loyalty proven by a simple cat—they settled back into the cold stone, waiting for the moon to signal their desperate move north.

Chapter 37: The Bothy's Silence

The bothy offered thin, desperate refuge. Its single room, built of rough, damp stone, did nothing to hold the bitter morning cold, but it provided absolute visual isolation. The space was utterly silent, save for the abrasive whisper of the wind scraping against the thick walls and the shallow, painful breathing of its two inhabitants. Scarlett used the fading daylight filtering through the gaps in the window stones to assess their damage.

AJ was slumped in the darkest corner, his posture broken, finally allowing his body to rest after the adrenaline dump. He was an officer of precise, controlled habit, and seeing him in such a state of physical and emotional ruin was more terrifying than any threat. His left shoulder was visibly purple, grossly distorted, and clearly dislocated. He was in profound, quiet pain, his face gray beneath the dirt and bruises.

"I need to put heat on that," Scarlett muttered, the medical urgency overriding the strategic. She rummaged through the small backpack they'd grabbed—a few sterile dressings, emergency energy bars, a detailed map of the Peaks, and a roll of black tactical tape. There were, critically, no painkillers.

"Arthur, the shoulder," she insisted, crawling toward him.

"No. Don't touch it," he managed, his voice a low, pained grate. "I can't risk you setting it wrong. We don't have enough leverage or strength to do it properly, and it'll just break again if we move. It's stable for now."

She accepted the limitation with a sharp intake of breath. Instead, she found a small, half-used tube of deep heat rub—a small miracle salvaged from the abandoned van. She gently massaged the cream around the swollen joint, avoiding direct pressure on the joint itself, working heat into the surrounding, shredded muscles. AJ groaned, biting down hard on his knuckles to muffle the sound, the effort of quiet endurance straining every muscle in his neck and jaw.

The Tactical Window

"The lie won us time," he finally whispered, the effort of speech drawing breath sharp with pain. He was referencing the "Fallow Ground" code he'd fed to Gary. "It means they'll pursue the internal threat, Drayton, which buys us a window before they realize the intelligence is fake. We gave Gary the right level of believable, high-stakes intel to consume his resources internally. But we are counting on a complex internal police sweep."

"And Gary?"

"Gary is currently consolidating. He has the operational name. He thinks he won the trade-off. But he'll predict that if we survived, we'll aim for the most isolated point. This bothy, this entire high-ground area, is effectively his trap. We have to use the terrain and move tonight. We can't stay past nightfall." He paused, his breathing shallow. "We have hours, maybe less, before Deedee starts putting together the pieces and realizes our extraction plan failed. We are running on borrowed time from two opposing forces."

He pulled a small, worn piece of paper from his tracksuit pocket—a tiny, faded picture of the two children, his niece and nephew. He held it tightly, smoothing the creases. "They're safe," he murmured, his voice softening slightly. "They're miles away. But Gary knows their location. I can't risk anything that brings attention back to them, even inadvertently, and that means zero communication until we're fully clear."

Financial Strategy and Rest

Scarlett's legal mind immediately engaged with the logistics. "We need to weaponize our anonymity. We need to become unfindable, not just by Gary's thugs, but by every uniformed officer on his payroll."

"We move by night, we stay hidden by day. We are the ghost operation now," AJ stated, his eyes dark with the strategy of evasion. "The goal is to get to a point where we can hit his finances, not his thugs. We need to freeze his assets, cripple his logistics—that's the only language a commander understands."

"And our legal status gives us leverage," Scarlett argued, her voice gaining strength. "If we can provide irrefutable evidence of Drayton and Gary's network—evidence outside the compromised Met unit—we become valuable witnesses, not wanted fugitives."

AJ nodded, a flicker of appreciation for her resilience crossing his face. "We are counting on the integrity of the system we both know is broken. We have to make ourselves too expensive to kill."

Scarlett nodded, crawling closer. She found the blanket from the bag and draped it over his shivering body. "Rest, Arthur. Just rest. I'll watch the door." She shifted, placing her hand near the cold steel of the pistol he had tucked away. "Your only job is to heal enough to stand up straight. We will move when it is safe. We will find Jade. We will get your life back." She settled beside him, holding the warmth of his body against hers, listening to the high, lonely sound of the wind and the absolute silence of the moorland. Their silence was the only security they possessed.

Chapter 38: The Ghost Operation

The bothy smelled of peat, damp stone, sweat, and despair. The air was cold, stinging their lungs. Scarlett woke abruptly, shivering uncontrollably, the rough wool of the blanket offering minimal warmth. AJ was already awake beside her, his breathing shallow and uneven, the sound a tight rasp in the profound darkness.

"Shoulder's locked up," he muttered, his voice strained and quiet. "It's seizing. I need you to tape it."

Scarlett didn't argue. She used the faint, metallic glow from the discarded pistol to locate the roll of black tactical tape in the backpack. She worked awkwardly, the cold stiffening her own bruised fingers, immobilizing his useless left arm tightly against his torso, creating a painful but essential sling. The process was silent save for AJ's sharp, involuntary intakes of breath.

"What's the plan?" she asked once the job was done, needing to impose order on the chaos inside her head.

"North Face," he muttered, using the military term for the coldest, most exposed, and often least-trafficked side of the mountain. "We move onto the high ground. Find a ridge that overlooks the main valleys. They'll search the roads first, they're predictable. We use the height for surveillance, watching the patrol patterns."

His voice grew firmer, reverting to the clipped, tactical rhythm she recognized from the raid. "No stopovers. Every minute we wait is a minute Gary's crew or a crooked uniform gets closer. We move slow, we move silent. We are a ghost operation now, Scarlett. We don't exist."

Assets and Liabilities

Scarlett leaned back against the stone wall, fighting the gnawing fatigue and the reality of their situation by imposing her own structure. She took a mental inventory of their assets:

Exhibit A: One stolen 9mm pistol (unknown ammo count, unknown provenance).

Exhibit B: £14.30 in coins and crumpled notes—their entire combined liquidity.

Exhibit C: One dislocated shoulder (AJ).

Exhibit D: One Barrister-in-training (Scarlett), wanted for murder.

"The only leverage we have is Jade. And Gary's bank accounts," she stated, listing the non-physical assets.

"Exactly. His finances are the key. He's running an entire ecosystem—moving bulk product, managing logistics, paying off half the city police, and buying his niece a new sofa. He has a complex financial structure," Scarlett mused, the lawyer in her finally finding a solvable puzzle. "We have to find an untraceable terminal—a dark web café or an unmonitored library computer—and start digging into his shell companies. If we can freeze or disrupt his cash flow, we can buy ourselves a window to get proper leverage."

"That requires risk," AJ acknowledged, pulling himself up, using the tactical tape as a lever. "We'll need to break cover, get a signal, and risk contact. And the first signal we send—will be to check on Jonesy."

"Jonesy?" Scarlett frowned, her voice breaking. "Arthur, we're talking about taking down a crime syndicate, and you're talking about the cat? They'd never waste time on him. What if he's still locked in your house, starving?"

AJ met her gaze, his dark eyes intense and steady, but holding a hint of the vulnerability she rarely saw. "I know, Scarlett. He's your family, and he's the only thing clean left in this mess. We need to know he's safe before we do anything else." He squeezed her hand. "And it's tactical. I told Deedee to secure him. If she followed that small, non-operational order, it proves she's loyal enough to receive the big intel. The cat is our test case for the entire Metropolitan Police, Scarlett." It was a deeply personal, rationalized line he was drawing, validating her emotional need through tactical logic.

He picked up the stolen pistol, testing its weight. "Let's walk, lawyer. We have a long night ahead, and we start by getting to that ridge."

Chapter 39: The High Ridge

The ascent onto the high ridge was agonizingly slow, conducted in the biting cold and the gray half-light of the moorland morning. AJ's left arm was plastered tightly against his chest by the black tactical tape, immobilizing his shoulder and making him look permanently half-drawn. Every uneven step was a conscious calculation against the searing pain. Scarlett moved ahead, her smaller frame navigating the treacherous, slippery terrain with more agility. She kept her focus outward, treating the hike like a forced reconnaissance mission.

"We need a name for Gary's financial anchor," Scarlett murmured, keeping her voice low against the wind. Her mind was already three steps ahead, back in the courtroom. "I know the legal structures—we need their Companies House registration details, Arthur. That's Exhibit A."

AJ dropped instantly behind a shelf of exposed rock, pausing to take a rasping, painful breath, scanning the valleys below. "We can't rest. If Deedee acted on the

Fallow Ground intel, Gary knows his operational information is compromised. He'll shift his assets, he'll disappear the mole—Drayton—and he'll deploy his local police assets to seal the Peaks."

He pushed himself up, leaning heavily on a walking stick he'd fashioned from a fallen branch. His eyes, though ringed with exhaustion, were burning with a desperate clarity. "The real assets are already liquid or disguised. The financial front will be his main weakness if we hit it quickly."

The Tactical Decision

"We need to risk the radio," AJ decided, the gravity of the statement immense. Breaking silence on a compromised network was the most dangerous thing they could do. "There's a high point nearby—Kinder Scout. It's too exposed, too visible, but it's the only place we'll get enough signal strength to break out of the immediate local network and reach Deedee's secondary scramble number again."

Scarlett consulted the map, her finger tracing the contours in the low light. "It's three hours away at your current speed, minimum. We risk exposure to every hiking group and farmer who decides to walk the summit, and we risk the signal being intercepted by Gary's radio assets."

"It's the best bad option," AJ countered, the phrase flat and emotionless. "We have to know if Jonesy is safe. That is the first condition."

Scarlett knew the sequence was non-negotiable. "If she didn't protect the cat, she won't protect the intel, and we pivot," she summarized. The logic was painful but sound: the highest-stakes test of loyalty rested on the fate of one ginger cat. "If he is safe, we tell her the financial front—that he must have used a central clearing agency or a high-end shell corporation to manage the bulk payments."

"Exactly. That gives Deedee's uncompromised team a target and buys us more time," AJ confirmed.

Legal Threats and Finality

"Fine. We move when the moon sets," Scarlett agreed, tucking the map back into the bag. The time felt arbitrary, but it gave them a goal. "But if a traffic cop sees us, I'm using my legal rights. I'm going to demand a solicitor and lodge a formal complaint against the police force of three counties. I will tie up every asset they commit to our pursuit with so much paperwork they can't move."

AJ actually managed a faint, bloody smile, a brief, startling flash of the man she had met at the rave. "You use your words, lawyer. You cause a magnificent, bureaucratic headache."

He tapped the pistol secured at his waist. "I'll use the gun to ensure you survive long enough to file the first subpoena." The statement wasn't a threat; it was a promise of brutal protection.

With the plan set—a dangerous climb, a high-risk radio call, and the fate of their entire resistance resting on the loyalty proven by a simple cat—they settled back into the cold stone, waiting for the moon to signal their desperate move north.

Chapter 40: The Price of Healing

The climb continued for another grueling hour, conducted in a strained, painful silence. Every step uphill exacerbated AJ's injuries. The black tactical tape securing his shoulder had begun to darken with seeped blood, and his teeth were clenched against a continuous, rattling tremor of pain that vibrated through his entire body.

"Shelter," AJ gasped, the word tasting like rust and exhaustion. He pulled them sharply off the faint trail, navigating instinctively toward a break in the rocky terrain. They found a substantial, abandoned stone barn—a perfect relic of the moorland past.

"We take the loft," AJ decided, his voice already weakening from the effort. "Better vantage, less visibility. If we can get off the ground, we can hear them coming."

Scarlett didn't need prompting. She knew this barn wasn't a stopover for rest; it was a makeshift field hospital. "Arthur, we need to address the arm now," she insisted, her professional detachment masking her deep fear. "You're burning up—the fever is starting. If we don't reduce the inflammation and realign the bone, you won't be able to climb Kinder Scout, and you certainly won't be able to use that arm for the fight."

"I know," he agreed, his eyes dull with acceptance. "But I'm not waiting for Deedee to send an ambulance that will just lead Gary straight to us. I have to set it myself, but I can't generate the opposing force." He pulled out the remaining two energy bars. "I need you to pull against my good arm. Lock my elbow. When I tell you, you pull hard, steady, and fast. Don't stop. Don't flinch. Do you understand, lawyer?"

The Command and the Contract

Scarlett's hands, though steady in court, were now shaking violently with cold and pure terror. She could see the grim resolution in his eyes. "Arthur, I don't think I can—"

"You're the only one here, Scarlett," he interrupted, his voice snapping with sharp, absolute authority that cut through the pain. "You are my asset. You are my command. You do not fail. Failure means we die in this barn. Compliance means we walk out."

She recognized the brutal necessity of the command. This was the contract of their shared fugitive life: he had the tactical knowledge and the survival skills; she had the will and the precision. She took a deep breath, fixing her gaze on the ceiling above his head, locking her shaking hands around his uninjured right arm, bracing herself against the cold stone floor.

"One." AJ's voice was a flat, preparatory warning.

"Two." He tensed, his entire body going rigid.

"Three!"

She pulled. She put her entire weight into the wrenching motion, pulling his arm straight and hard, resisting the natural instinct to flinch or ease the pressure.

A sound ripped from AJ's chest that defied human language—a thick, strangled, "FUUUUCK!" followed by a primal bellow of agony that was instantly cut short as he bit down hard on his tongue.

Scarlett felt a sickening thunk deep in her own shoulder, the sympathetic pain mirroring the trauma, followed by the wet, grinding sound of the bone sliding back into its socket. AJ collapsed against the wall, utterly silent, his eyes squeezed shut, breathing in shallow, ragged bursts.

Temporary Victory

"It's in, you massive git," he finally managed to whisper, the insult delivered with profound gratitude and relief. "It's in. Now we tape."

Scarlett, fighting down the nausea and the residual shock, quickly immobilized the joint, taping the arm firmly and cleanly against his torso. The realignment was rough, but effective.

"We sleep for three hours," AJ instructed, his voice low and depleted but regaining its strength. "The cold will help the swelling. Then we move." He pulled her down onto the straw beside him, his strong, recently abused right arm wrapping around her waist. His body was a map of contradictions: broken, yet intensely protective. "We have a fighting chance now, Scarlett. Go to sleep."

She held the warmth of his body against hers, listening to the wind and the silence. The dislocated shoulder was fixed. The lie was set. They had survived the price of healing.

Chapter 41: Ghosts and Memories

Scarlett lay pressed against AJ's good side, the coarse, damp straw scratching her skin through the borrowed hoodie. Her body was a rigid map of aches and stitches, but the sharp, raw memory of the bone grinding in its socket during the reduction made sleep impossible. She listened intently to the aggressive wind tearing at the stone walls and focused on the steady, rhythmic drum of AJ's heart—a fragile, precious counterpoint to the terrifying silence of the Peak District.

Her mind inevitably retreated, seeking refuge in the week they had stolen—a brief, luminous flash of normalcy set against this cold, brutal reality. She smiled faintly, remembering the chaotic, pure joy of the kitchen confrontation, or him simply making coffee. The fantasy of their wedding flashed behind her eyelids: *He would wear a simple suit, probably dark gray. We'd get married somewhere small, overlooking the sea, and I'd still wear my battered black Converse under the dress.* The clarity of the imagined future was overwhelming. But the fantasies were gone now, replaced by the grim, sickening reality that if they ever survived this, there would be no clean wedding, no simple future—only the legal fallout of murder and internal corruption.

A small, sharp sound, utterly foreign to the natural soundscape of the wind and the rustling straw, ripped through her reflection. Clink-clink-clink. Scarlett went instantly rigid, her breath catching in her throat. AJ's breathing changed immediately—shallow, silent, the trained cessation of sound she had learned to recognize.

The sound came again: a rhythmic, metallic clink-clink-clink echoing from the uneven rocks outside the barn.

AJ's strong right hand clamped instantly over her mouth, his grip a silent order to move, to be silent. His eyes, even in the gloom, were wide and focused. He knew what it was. A tracker. A piece of police equipment—or something even more sinister—dropped in the rocks to mark their position.

"Copper," a rough voice shouted, amplified by the high wind, yet muffled slightly by the thick stone walls. "We know you're in there. We saw the abandoned van half a mile back. Come out now, or we burn the whole bloody thing down."

The Cornered Asset

"Three of them," AJ whispered against her ear, his lips brushing the shell of her ear. His breath was warm, but his voice was cold, precise. "All wearing standard issue uniform. They're doing Gary's cleanup for him."

Scarlett's heart hammered so fiercely she thought the sound alone would betray them. They were cornered; the entire local police force was effectively the enemy.

AJ thumbed the safety off the pistol. The soft click of the mechanism was deafening in the silence. "When I move, you take the rope and get into the loft opening," he instructed, his tactical mind cutting through the pain. "Don't move, don't breathe, until I signal." He was forcing her into the pre-planned hiding space.

"Arthur, no," she mouthed silently against his hand, her eyes wide with desperate protest. She knew his one good arm and damaged body were no match for three armed men, even if they were just traffic cops.

"The loft, Scarlett," he hissed, his eyes locked on the door. "That's an order." He was reverting to absolute command, shutting down their partnership to protect her.

The local officer kicked the wooden door once, the impact splintering the old wood with a deafening crack that shook the entire structure. "Last chance, Bonnie! Send the copper out, or we start using the thermals!"

AJ's hand slid from her mouth to the small of her back, pushing her toward the dark, elevated opening above them. He was forcing her into the role of the passive asset, the witness who survives. She felt the rope he'd secured earlier dig into her hand.

She had the pistol, but she knew AJ, injured as he was, was setting himself up as the bait. His life was the immediate trade for her survival. The brutal simplicity of his command—*The loft, Scarlett. That's an order*—left her with no choice but to obey, even as every instinct screamed at her to fight beside him.

Chapter 42: The Bait and the Switch

The main barn door splintered under the force of the officer's kick, confirming the absolute, lethal intent of the people outside. They were executing an arrest warrant that carried a death sentence.

"Arthur, please," Scarlett whispered, grabbing his uninjured arm, her voice shaking but desperate to sound tactical. "We take the back way. We don't fight three men with one gun and a broken arm."

"There is no back way," AJ grated out, his eyes fixed on the door that was now bowing inward. The stone walls were too thick, the window too small. "This is the only door. We play the hand we've been dealt."

"Five seconds, mate, or we come in hot!" the lead officer shouted again, the term *mate* making the threat sound chillingly familiar and local.

AJ moved with startling, desperate speed, but not toward the entrance. He shoved the pistol hard into

Scarlett's hands. The cold steel was a shocking weight against her palm. "You know how to use this. You cover the window. I'm the distraction." He then grabbed a large, half-full feed sack from the corner, the coarse burlap scratching against his skin.

"The second they open that door," AJ instructed, his voice low and intense, drilling the orders into her mind, "you climb, and you don't look back. And don't shoot unless they aim at me. Don't kill them; they're police assets, not the network."

"I'm not leaving you!" Scarlett hissed, the thought of abandoning him causing a white-hot spike of panic.

"You're the only one who can get to Gary's finances," AJ countered, his gaze burning with finality. "You are my objective. Your brain is the asset. My life is expendable. Now, loft!"

The Diversion

Scarlett obeyed, the trained soldier in her recognizing the necessary sacrifice. She scrambled desperately up the rope and onto the rickety ladder into the hayloft, the coarse straw hiding her from the main entrance.

The main door groaned, then burst inward under a final, heavy impact, revealing three uniformed officers, their bodies silhouetted against the morning light.

"Show us your hands! On the floor!" the plainclothes officer shouted, his voice tight with anticipation.

AJ roared, a fierce, guttural battle cry of a wounded animal. He threw the heavy feed sack hard across the room, mimicking the weight and trajectory of a body. The feed exploded in a cloud of dust and straw, momentarily blinding the officers and choking the small, confined space. The air was instantly thick, confusing their thermal imaging. AJ launched himself directly at the nearest officer, using the distraction to close the distance.

"Go! Go!" AJ yelled, locked in a desperate, single-armed struggle, his taped shoulder absorbing a terrible, wrenching stress. He was fighting only to consume time, to buy her seconds.

Scarlett didn't hesitate. Her survival instinct, honed by a week of pure fear and tactical necessity, took over. She scrambled across the loft floor to a narrow gap in the stone wall—a space she and AJ had identified as a final escape route. She hauled her smaller frame through the tight opening, the rough stone tearing at the borrowed tracksuit. She hit the cold, mossy ground of the coombe, rolling instantly to avoid detection, the pistol digging painfully into her side.

The Silence

She didn't look back. She could hear the muffled, brutal sounds of the fight inside—the thuds of bodies, the heavy impact of a baton, and AJ's ragged breathing—then a sudden, strained silence.

Her mind flashed back to AJ's final, urgent, self-sacrificing order: *You are my objective.* She started to run, keeping low, using the rising sun to guide her, heading blindly toward the highest point on the map. She had to get to Kinder Scout.

The wind carried the last sound from the barn—a sharp, sickening CRACK that was instantly followed by an absolute, final silence. He was gone.

She ran harder, faster, the loss a sharp, new engine of vengeance. She was alone again, the pistol and the mission to expose Gary's financial network now her only anchor. She was the ghost operation now.

Chapter 43: The Signal

Scarlett ran until the pain in her thigh became a steady, rhythmic torture, an anchor against the rising, hysterical panic. She scrambled up the steepest incline she could find, putting as much vertical distance as possible between herself and the silent stone barn. The wind howled around her, carrying away the last echoes of the violent confrontation. AJ was gone—captured, incapacitated, or worse. The sickening *CRACK* that had preceded the silence was now etched into her memory.

She finally collapsed behind a massive rock outcrop, her lungs burning, the taste of blood and dust metallic on her tongue. The cold granite felt grounding. She retrieved the tiny, cheap burner phone AJ had given her. She had one chance to make this call before the network triangulated the transmission.

She dialed Deedee's private scramble number. The phone rang three times. Then, a sharp, professional click.

"This is Deedee."

"Deedee, it's Scarlett Harper. I'm on Kinder Scout. Arthur is... he's been captured. The local police are working with Gary's network. They tried to take us at the barn."

Deedee's voice remained perfectly level, betraying nothing. "Jacobs is captured? Location?"

"Unknown. But he confirmed the mole—Drayton, the analyst. You got Drayton, didn't you? Did you manage to hit the plant?" Scarlett's voice shook, demanding confirmation of the internal threat.

"We moved. Drayton is in custody. Your intel was critical for that. Thank you." Deedee confirmed the only good news, but held back further operational details.

The Jonesy Test and Final Intel

Scarlett ignored the confirmation of success. Her priority shifted to the trust test. "I have the current operational code Gary believes is authentic. Before I transmit that, or any financial targets, I need proof you are not compromised."

"Ms. Harper, we just confirmed the mole and acted on your intel."

"No," Scarlett countered, her voice dropping to a low, cold challenge that demanded absolute, personal honesty. "Not until I know if you're clean. You have three seconds. Jonesy. Is the cat safe?"

A beat of absolute, terrifying silence stretched across the compromised network. Then, Deedee's voice returned, measured and controlled, but with a subtle new weight of respect. "The animal is a ginger tabby. It was retrieved from your new-build address and is currently secure. It refuses to eat any food that isn't poultry-based kibble."

"Good." The relief was immense, allowing Scarlett to trust the line. "Listen closely. The plant was a decoy. They cleared out the high-value product hours before we arrived. Arthur gave Gary a false operational code: Fallow Ground. It's fake, but it bought us time. Gary is consolidating. His financial front is [redacted: property management name]. You won't break him with thugs; you break him with bank secrecy and money laundering. That's the real core."

"Financial warfare. I understand," Deedee confirmed.

The New Objective

"I need eyes on his transport and detention points. I'm not leaving the area. Arthur is hurt, and Gary is using him for counterintelligence. He needs to know I'm still functional."

"Ms. Harper, that is reckless. You need immediate extraction."

"No. I'm his leverage, Deedee," Scarlett countered, the words sharp with tactical realization. "And right now, I'm his best distraction. You hit the property firms. You go for the ledger, Dee. You cut the head off the snake."

Scarlett ended the call, smashing the cheap phone against the granite rock, the sound surprisingly loud in the vast silence of the Peaks. The glass shattered, ensuring no tracking was possible. She stood alone on the ridge, the cold wind whipping around her, the pistol heavy in her hand. Her grief was deferred. Her mission was clear.

Chapter 44: The Descent

Scarlett didn't wait for the cold to fully set in. The moment she ended the call with Deedee, she smashed the small burner phone against a piece of jagged granite. The sharp, violent sound of shattering plastic and glass was final and absolute, tearing the silence of the high ridge. The call had cost her the safety of electronic silence, but in exchange, she'd gained critical, verified intelligence: Jonesy was safe, and Deedee was clean enough to trust.

She found a small, sheer crevice in the tor where the aggressive wind wasn't quite so brutal. Pulling out the detailed map, her mind shifted entirely to tactical survival. The narcotic fog had lifted entirely, leaving a heightened, painful clarity—she was functioning purely on adrenaline and a terrifying urgency.

Adversary Inventory

She forced herself to analyze the situation from a position of detached, legalistic logic, listing her adversaries and their capabilities:

- Gary's Network: Armed, motivated, and now searching the high ground. Their intent was recapture and elimination.
- Corrupt Local Police: The immediate, most confusing threat. They were the visible institution of justice, but they were hunting her as a killer. Their primary job was to lock down the area and execute Gary's capture order.
- Deedee's Unit: The uncertain ally. Too constrained by protocol and corruption to offer immediate aid, but they held the keys to Gary's destruction via his finances.

She was operating in a lethal tri-polar conflict, and she was the smallest variable.

The Agony of Movement

With the plan set, she started the slow, agonizing descent. Her target wasn't random; it was a series of rough, dry stone walls she identified on the map—natural cover that ran along a high, isolated sheep track. Every downward step sent a fresh jolt of pain through her bruised ribs and the stitched wound on her stomach. The terrain was unforgiving; slippery shale and wet moss made the descent treacherous, forcing her to rely on the pistol's weight for balance.

The moorland air was dense and cold, smelling of wet earth and distant peat fires. The utter silence was the most terrifying element, amplifying every sound she made—the scrape of her shoe, the rustle of her borrowed tracksuit.

Mid-morning, just as the sun began to break through the cloud cover, the absolute silence was ripped apart by the distant, muffled sound of a police siren. The sound wasn't close, but it was relentless, echoing off the valley walls. They were sweeping the main roads below the moorland.

She stayed motionless for nearly twenty minutes, pressing herself flat against the cold earth behind a large boulder. She closed her eyes, forcing herself to focus on the sound's direction, waiting for it to cycle away. The realization was stark: the local police weren't searching the ridge yet; they were locking down the escape routes, cutting off the low ground. It was containment, executed with chilling precision, exactly as AJ had predicted.

The Path North

She moved only when absolutely necessary, finding the sheep track just as the morning wore on. The track offered easier passage north, leading toward a cluster of isolated farms marked on the map. She held onto the hope that farms meant potential shelter, maybe water, and perhaps a chance to get eyes on the news—her only way to know if Gary had started the final, public stage of his operation against AJ.

She paused at a dry stone wall, her breath coming in visible puffs of vapor. She was exhausted, battered, and utterly alone, the emotional weight of AJ's capture a crushing deferral of grief. But she was alive, and she was moving. Her survival was no longer accidental; it was a cold, calculated campaign against the impossible odds.

She adjusted the pistol, nestled securely in her waistband, and set her face toward the horizon. Her mind was clear: the lawyer was now an operative. She had to find him.

Chapter 45: Return from the Dead

The sheep track, running along the spine of the exposed moorland, eventually led Scarlett into a shallow, wooded valley. The change in terrain offered the first true cover since she abandoned the van. Tucked away amongst a stand of gnarled, wind-battered oaks, she spotted a derelict shooting hut – little more than a stone shell with a collapsed roof and a gaping doorway.

She stumbled inside, the coarse, wet stone floor a relief after the long miles of rough terrain. Her last reserves of adrenaline drained away, leaving her hollowed out and shivering. Her teeth were chattering uncontrollably, and her hands were so numb she could barely unclip the pistol from her waistband. The wind whistled mournfully through the broken rafters. The thought of AJ, captured and interrogated, was a dull, constant throb behind her eyes, a deferred grief that had kept her running.

A sharp snap of a twig outside the hut jolted her fully awake. The sound was too close, too distinct to be the wind or a foraging animal. She scrambled for the pistol, her fingers clumsy and frozen, fumbling the safety mechanism. The dark silhouette of a man appeared, blocking the last sliver of daylight in the doorway.

Scarlett's breath hitched, turning into a ragged, silent plea. She raised the pistol, planting her feet wide, fighting the narcotic residue and fatigue with sheer terror. "Stay back!" she croaked, her voice dry and unfamiliar. "I'll shoot! I swear to God, I'll shoot!"

The figure froze instantly, remaining silhouetted against the weak light. "Scarlett. Stop. It's me." The voice was rough, ragged, laced with pain, but utterly unmistakable.

"Arthur?" she whispered, the name a fractured sound of disbelief. "No. You're... you're not real. They had you. I heard the crack. I heard the silence."

"They had me," AJ confirmed, stepping cautiously into the hut, his hands raised in the universal gesture of surrender. The movement was slow, deliberate. "But not for long. You're faster than you look, lawyer. Too fast, in fact. You left me for dead, you little shit." The teasing insult, delivered with profound exhaustion, was the most real sound she had heard in hours.

The Cost of Freedom

He looked utterly destroyed. The borrowed tracksuit was torn and smeared with fresh mud, oil, and blood. A deep, jagged cut bled sluggishly above his left eyebrow, and his taped left arm hung low and still, clearly useless. He moved with the staggered, careful gait of someone whose body was entirely failing them.

"How?" Scarlett finally managed, lowering the pistol slightly, though she didn't put it down. The simple question was freighted with the events of the barn, the sound of the crack, and the sheer impossibility of his freedom.

"The police are not trained for close-quarters unarmed combat when they expect a simple walk-in arrest," AJ explained, his voice low and tactical, even now. "And a dislocated shoulder is only a problem if you don't intend to use it as a weapon. I forced the dislocation further to buy separation from the first officer. The *CRACK* you heard was my desperate way of getting leverage." He paused, breathing deeply. "I got out. Then I followed your tracks."

He walked over to her, closing the final, painful distance. He knelt, not in supplication, but because he could no longer stand easily. He then simply wrapped his good right arm around her, pulling her close, burying his face in the hood of her borrowed tracksuit. "I thought... I heard the final sound of them dragging you away..." she stammered, reliving the terror.

"I know," he murmured, his voice muffled against her shoulder. "I know. I made some noise getting out." The lie was obvious, designed to shield her from the truth of her temporary abandonment, but in that moment, she accepted it entirely.

He held her tightly, transmitting a desperate, raw relief that mirrored her own. They were still hunted, still broken, still wanted for murder, but now, they were together again, huddled in a freezing stone ruin. And the fight, against all odds, was back on.

Chapter 46: Borrowed Time

AJ checked the area surrounding the dilapidated shooting hut, moving slowly but methodically, his actions hampered by the constant, grinding pain in his shoulder. The moment of reunion was over; the operational clock was ticking. "We have to move," AJ rasped, leaning against the cold stone doorframe. "We need elevation and a source of supplies. We can't survive on straw and tactical tape."

Scarlett was already taking inventory of their medical needs, tearing the sleeve from her massive grey hoodie. "We need to address your shoulder properly, Arthur. That tape is just holding it in the wrong position, and you know it. But before that, we need food and heat. We have fourteen pounds and thirty pence." The meager sum was a shocking representation of their total worth.

"There's a large, isolated farm marked on the map, about three miles north," AJ said, his voice flat. "Too close to risk a direct approach. We find a small village.

We risk the last of our cash on clean clothes and high-calorie food."

She traced a finger across a smaller mark on the map. "Edale. It's closer to the major trails. Fewer residents, but still has a shop and maybe a pub. It's a calculated risk—we blend in with the hikers. We look like we had a rough night camping."

"Edale it is," AJ conceded, nodding his immediate approval. "We move before sunrise. Stay off the marked trails and use the shadows and high ground."

The Descent and the Disguise

As the pale light of the sun began to filter over the rugged peaks, they reached the outskirts of the small village. They looked like creatures dragged straight from the earth: bruised, mud-caked, and pale. They found a concealed spot near the shallow river and used the icy water to clean the worst of the grime and dried blood from their faces and hands. The cold was a sharp, painful jolt, but necessary.

"I go in," Scarlett decided, the logic obvious. She was less physically marked by the recent torture than AJ was by the constant pain and the visible damage to his arm. "I look less suspicious. You look like you're one dislocated shoulder away from a prison break. I need to buy us at least two days of high-calorie food, a first-aid kit to properly clean our wounds, and new clothes. I can't walk around in this oversized hoodie anymore."

"I need you to be invisible," AJ cautioned, his eyes boring into hers. "You are our lifeline. No eye contact. No credit cards. Pay only with change. If you see a police patrol, you abort and run. Do not engage." He handed her the entire £14.30.

The Shattered Anonymity

Scarlett walked into the small, brightly lit general store. The air was warm, smelling of fresh bread and coffee—a stark, painful contrast to the damp cold of the bothy. She kept her eyes focused on the shelves, trying to look like a slightly disoriented backpacker. She managed to buy two rolls, trail mix, water, antiseptic, thick hiking socks, and a cheap, massive, waterproof poncho designed to hide the bulk of AJ's injured shoulder. She emptied her entire cash reserve onto the counter—the transactional end of their life as fugitives.

Just as the cashier bagged the items, the small television mounted high in the corner of the shop caught her eye. It was running a national news bulletin. The screen showed a grainy, poorly enlarged photo of AJ's face, followed instantly by her own, the picture clearly taken from her old social media profile. The ticker tape graphic across the bottom of the screen read in bold, flashing red: "FUGITIVES. ARMED AND EXTREMELY DANGEROUS."

"Terrible, isn't it, dear?" the cashier said, glancing back at Scarlett, completely oblivious to the person standing before her. "That handsome young man and his poor girlfriend. Looks like something right out of a movie."

"Yes," Scarlett managed, her voice tight and distant. "Terrible."

She grabbed the bag and walked out of the shop. The anonymity of Edale, of the Peak District, and of the entire country was shattered. The whole world knew their faces and their story—the false story created by Gary's network. She was no longer just running from Gary's thugs; she was running from the perception of the world.

Chapter 47: The Next Move

The anonymity of Edale had vanished, replaced by the crushing weight of national exposure. Scarlett walked quickly but smoothly, forcing her rising panic down beneath a professional veneer. The image of their faces—Arthur's haunted, her own bruised—staring out from the national news confirmed their lethal status: they were the most wanted couple in the UK.

She slipped behind the ancient stone pub, finding AJ tucked behind a high, dense gorse bush near the riverbank. The scent of wet leaves and earth was strong, a temporary mask for the stench of fear and adrenaline.

"It's everywhere," she confirmed, showing him the bag of supplies. "National news. They're painting us as the Bonnie and Clyde of the Peaks. Disgraced officer, accomplice lawyer, murdering drug dealers. They know we're armed."

AJ absorbed the news without visible reaction, his face a mask of controlled fatigue. "Good," he said, the statement sounding clinically insane. "Massive exposure means the London unit will have to get involved, pulling the focus away from the corrupt local patrols. Deedee can work better in the chaos when the official narrative is high-profile. She'll get jurisdiction."

"The bad news is this pub and the entire valley are now risks," Scarlett countered, her voice low. "They'll start plastering notices locally, and every hiker will be watching for the *Bonnie and Clyde* car. The locals are effectively hostile now, whether they're police or not."

He took the supplies, his good hand instantly checking the inventory. "Antiseptic, food, dark socks, and the poncho. Perfect." He checked the map again, his finger tracing a new vector. "We move deeper into the moors, towards the Pennine Way. High traffic, but also high visibility. We need to create a trail of confusion and blend in with the genuine hikers."

"We use the crowd," Scarlett agreed, finding the logic immediately soothing. "We hike. We look exhausted, miserable, and normal for the Peaks in November. We blend in until we can secure a new base further north."

The Objective Shift: Financial Warfare

"We need leverage. We need something so valuable that Gary is forced to move his assets, giving Deedee the opening she needs," AJ stated, his priority absolute: crippling the network was secondary only to keeping Scarlett alive. "Our physical survival is entirely dependent on our ability to create maximum financial pressure."

"The money," Scarlett whispered, recognizing the tactical wisdom. "The financial structure. I'm a solicitor, Arthur. I know how to track money laundering through Companies House and bank records. Gary isn't moving cash in briefcases; he's moving it through shell entities. That is the weak point."

"Exactly. We don't have the manpower to fight his thugs, but you have the legal knowledge to dismantle his entire logistics network," AJ affirmed. "But tracking that requires time, secure access, and a functioning terminal. This is where your skills replace my own."

"We move north toward the next village, Hayfield," AJ decided, folding the map. "It's further, but it's a better position to pivot into urban areas if we need to access a terminal, and it keeps us off the immediate sweep pattern of the local patrols."

"We stick to the high ground, we walk until sunset, and we do not stop for anyone." He looked at her, his dark eyes intense. The plan was set.

The New Reality

Scarlett watched a young couple in brightly colored hiking gear walk past the pub, their laughter echoing the life she no longer possessed. She pulled the large, dark poncho from the bag and handed it to AJ. He slipped it over his massive frame and his taped shoulder, the dark fabric instantly disguising his injury and turning him into a single, anonymous silhouette of a hiker caught in the rain.

They emerged from the gorse bush and started walking, deliberately choosing the well-trodden path. Every step felt like a lie. They were murderers in the eyes of the public, and every person they passed was a potential informer. The true battle wasn't with Gary's thugs in the dark; it was with the national narrative running on the television screens and the institutional corruption poisoning the local force.

"Every person is a risk, every car is a threat," AJ murmured, his voice low enough to be lost in the wind. "We hold our nerve, and we get to Hayfield."

Their survival clock was ticking down to their next desperate move: risking exposure to find a computer and launch financial warfare against a man who believed he owned the law.

Chapter 48: The Cost of Isolation

The low, pale light of early morning was their enemy, making every rock and shadow a potential target for surveillance. AJ forced them to move off the vulnerable valley floor and scramble onto a rough, concealed path paralleling the Pennine Way. The wide, open sky provided zero cover. AJ was wrapped entirely in the oversized dark poncho, the fabric successfully concealing his bulky, taped shoulder, while Scarlett, favoring her bruised ribs, moved with a controlled, pained stiffness.

"We need a new cover story," Scarlett muttered, keeping her voice low against the wind. Her solicitor's mind worked on creating a plausible defense for their appearance.

"If we meet anyone," AJ instructed, scanning the horizon, "we're a search party. Lost contact with a friend who was walking the high trails. No names. Keep the story simple and avoid eye contact."

AJ stopped abruptly, his body dropping instantly. "Down. Fast!" he hissed, pressing himself flat behind a low outcrop of shale.

A large, dark police helicopter crested the ridge opposite, its rotors beating the air with a heavy, purposeful rhythm. The machine wasn't sweeping randomly; it was running a grid search. "They're using thermal imaging," AJ whispered against the cold stone, his voice taut with recognition. "They know we're on the moors."

The Betrayal of the Ally

The helicopter lingered for a minute, its thermal signature potentially painting them as fugitives, before moving on. AJ watched it disappear. "That wasn't local," AJ stated, pushing himself up slowly. "That's specialized hardware. That's not the corrupt local force looking for Bonnie and Clyde."

Scarlett understood instantly. "Deedee's unit is running the distraction of the local corruption to run their own silent sweep, trying to find us before Gary's people do."

"Exactly. The mole (Drayton) is already arrested, but the rest of the Met doesn't know the scale of the corruption yet. Deedee's clean team is running that thermal sweep, trying to retrieve me before the local police—Gary's people—can eliminate me. I'm a witness to the whole thing."

"So we'll be taken by both sides of the law," Scarlett concluded, the realization cold and absolute.

"We need to risk a car," AJ decided, his strategic thinking accelerating. "Walking is too slow for this radius of search. We can't evade a thermal sweep on foot."

The Cottage and the Fire

They found a small, unnamed valley, dropping into a rare pocket of concealment. Tucked against the side of the hill, nearly invisible beneath thick ivy and gorse, was a dilapidated, but intact stone cottage. The roof sagged, but the walls stood firm.

"We take five minutes of heat," AJ instructed, pulling the flint and steel from the supply bag. He handed them to Scarlett. "You start the fire."

"And what the fuck do you expect me to do with this, Bear Grylls?" she snapped back, the fear and exhaustion breaking through into frustration. The tools were foreign to her metropolitan life.

"You rub the steel against the flint. You create a spark. You light the tinder. It's the most basic survival skill there is. You've never even camped, have you?"

"I am an Associate Solicitor! I order Deliveroo! My survival skills involve knowing which court clerk to bribe!" she snapped, but she dropped to the floor, her pride warring with necessity.

She eventually managed to start a small, smoky fire using dry grass and splintered wood, the smoke an inherent risk but the warmth an immediate necessity. She then carefully unwrapped AJ's shoulder.

"Arthur," she said, her voice dropping to a serious, low tone. "We can't keep moving with just this stick and three bullets. We need money, a vehicle, and a plan that gets us out of the Peaks. We need to hit Gary's finances now."

"We need to risk Manchester," AJ finally conceded, the word heavy with risk.

"It's suicide," Scarlett whispered, thinking of the high concentration of police and CCTV.

"It's the only place we can find the high-grade terminal access you need to start digging into Gary's property firms. It's the highest risk, but it has the greatest reward. We go in, we hit the ledger, and we disappear again."

Chapter 49: The Manchester Run

AJ spent the next three grueling hours preparing, not by resting, but by analyzing the patrol patterns and the wind direction from their hidden vantage point. His concentration was absolute, a final defense against the exhaustion and pain. "The helicopter sweep confirms they think we're still deep in the rural zone," AJ stated, his voice a low, gravelly whisper. "We rely on that assumption. We go into the city, fast, before they shift resources from the local sweep to urban lockdown."

"We're looking for an isolated communication nexus—somewhere untraceable, preferably hardwired," Scarlett confirmed, shivering. They needed speed, but they needed security more. The thought of exposing themselves to Manchester's ubiquitous CCTV network felt like diving into a shark tank.

They waited forty agonizing minutes, huddled in the cold brush, before AJ's patience paid off. A battered Vauxhall Corsa, looking completely ordinary and out of place, pulled into a passing point nearby. The sole driver—a middle-aged man checking his phone—stepped out briefly to stretch his legs, providing the window AJ required.

AJ moved instantly. He crossed the broken ground with silent, economical speed, the sudden action tearing a moan from his lips, quickly suppressed. The driver slumped soundlessly against the car frame, neutralized by a single, precise strike to the neck. "Keys," AJ commanded, returning a moment later, already pulling the dark poncho off his shoulder. "He'll be out for twenty minutes. Enough time to hide him and be gone in the Corsa."

Peak to Concrete

They quickly transferred to the Corsa, the small cabin offering a jarring contrast to the vast, cold moor. They secured the driver, ensuring the immediate area was clean, and wiped down the Corsa's surfaces as best they could. As AJ navigated the winding peak roads, the sense of isolation slowly gave way to the overwhelming density of the approaching metropolis. The air thickened with humidity and diesel fumes. The contrast was a necessary, strategic shock.

"Gary's financial front has to be property," Scarlett recited, her voice steady against the engine noise. "I need to get into the Companies House and Land Registry databases. I have to cross-reference directors and subsidiaries to find his shell corporations. That requires several hours of dedicated, untraceable terminal time—nothing we can risk on a public connection."

"I know a place," AJ interrupted, easing the Corsa onto the main motorway, seamlessly merging with the traffic. "An old army contact runs a data recovery firm in the city center. It's secure, off the grid, and he owes me a major favor. He won't ask questions."

Scarlett nodded, the pieces of their final tactical loop clicking into place. "Your debriefing procedure code, 'Fallow Ground,' is meaningless, but it tells Gary two things," she mused. "One, you prioritize protecting the unit over your life—which confirms his theory that you are compromised but still loyal to the Met."

"Two, Deedee is communicating with you. When Gary realizes the 'Fallow Ground' intel is fake—and he will—he'll shift his focus entirely to proving Deedee is corrupt. He'll commit resources to her takedown."

The Final Gamble

"That buys us the time to hit the financial heart," AJ concluded, the logic grim but necessary. "We hit the finances, give the proof to Deedee, and she brings the entire institutional weight of national law enforcement down on Gary, bypassing the local corruption." The high-risk gamble depended on perfect timing and Deedee's integrity.

Scarlett looked out the window as the landscape transformed from rock and sheep to endless rows of terraced houses and industrial parks. Manchester was swallowing them. She was no longer just the lawyer; she was the active operative in this final gambit.

"We need to risk Manchester," AJ finally conceded, the word heavy with risk and finality.

"It's suicide," Scarlett whispered, thinking of the high concentration of police and CCTV, the millions of potential witnesses running their faces.

"It's the only place we can find the high-grade terminal access you need to start digging into Gary's property firms. It's the highest risk, but it has the greatest reward. We go in, we hit the ledger, and we disappear again." Their window was closing fast, and their desperate run into the heart of the city was their only path left.

Chapter 50: The Arthur Jacobs Story

The Vauxhall Corsa was unremarkable, a dull gray shield carrying two fugitives deeper into the relentless flow of traffic into Manchester. Scarlett, ignoring the frantic pace of the motorway, was meticulously re-reading the single sheet of paper—AJ's suspension letter—her barrister's training seeking a loophole, a defense, anything that could restore the man beside her.

"Arthur," she said quietly, folding the paper with precision. "What did you do in the army that led you here? You said Special Reconnaissance, but what does that mean, exactly? The way you move... the way you fight..."

AJ kept his eyes focused on the endless stream of headlights, his posture stiff against the pain in his shoulder. "I was Arthur in the army," he started, his voice flat. "Ten years. Special Reconnaissance (SR). My job wasn't frontline combat; it was deep observation, intelligence gathering, and non-sanctioned extraction, often hundreds of miles behind enemy lines. I was a ghost. I operated alone. In that world, emotional attachment isn't a benefit; it's liability."

"My last tour didn't end well," he continued, the silence growing heavy with implied history. "Deedee's unit—Specialist Crime—they scout guys like me. Broken assets who know how to disappear. My job for the last year was to maintain the cover identity of Arthur Jacobs, tree surgeon and part-time DJ, and feed intelligence on the OCGs (Organized Crime Groups) running the network."

Scarlett finally lowered the paperwork, acknowledging the impossible truth. "So, you are genetically predisposed to being a ghost, Arthur. And I, your liability, blew up your ten years of impeccable cover within a single week."

"You didn't blow anything up, Scarlett," AJ countered, his voice surprisingly firm. "You exposed a weakness I didn't know I had. And you gave Deedee's unit the key they've been missing for years—Gary's central command. Before you, he was just a mid-level dealer. Now we know he's the commander of a sophisticated criminal network."

The Manchester Gambit

The silence returned, broken only by the sharp, low thrum of the engine. The gravity of their current situation pressed down on them.

"The owner of this Corsa reported it stolen an hour after I neutralized him," AJ stated, shifting seamlessly from backstory to tactical reality. "It's already flagged on ANPR (Automatic Number Plate Recognition) cameras. We have maybe fifteen minutes in this car before it pings an alert near the city centre, and that ping goes straight to the local patrol cars that Gary controls."

Scarlett checked her own watch. "Fifteen minutes to reach your contact, get inside, and disappear from the street grid."

"Exactly," AJ affirmed. "We're leveraging the assumption that because we're professional, we wouldn't commit the obvious suicide of driving a stolen vehicle directly into a major metropolitan area. Gary's biggest blind spot is his ego. He's counting on the fact that the only person who knows his full financial structure is a disgraced ex-operative and a drugged-up solicitor."

"He believes his containment is absolute. He thinks we're broken and running for our lives, not running for his bank accounts." Scarlett felt a cold, determined resolve settle over her. "We hit the finances, prove we're more than just Bonnie and Clyde, and force him to panic."

The Last Command

AJ took a hand off the wheel and squeezed her knee, a final, necessary moment of connection before they dove into the hostile city. "This is it, Scarlett. This is the last risk. I need you to understand the danger. This contact is clean, but the moment you start digging, the fire spreads. We go in, we extract the information, and we leave."

"I understand. We hit the ledger," she affirmed. "And we prove that a woman who orders Deliveroo can still bring down a system built on corruption."

"We move now," AJ said, his eyes scanning the looming skyscrapers of the city ahead. "The ghost and the lawyer. Let's finish this."

Chapter 51: The Moment of Stillness

The Vauxhall Corsa shuddered to a final, violent halt in a shadowy, multi-storey car park near the city's financial district. The air was heavy with the smell of stale exhaust and cold concrete. The engine was instantly killed, plunging the small cabin into a tense silence. "Fifteen minutes, maximum," AJ muttered, his voice tight. "The ANPR alert is active. Every patrol car in a three-mile radius is looking for this license plate."

Scarlett was slumped against the passenger door, her mind a cold landscape of loss: no home, no job, no future, and officially branded a murderer on every news channel. The exhaustion was immense, but the adrenaline remained, a thin, painful shield.

AJ didn't immediately move toward the door. He turned to her, his dark eyes intense, searching her face for a sign of collapse. "We just faced down death twice, you watched me set my own bone, and you ran from three armed officers alone," he said, his voice dropping to a low, raw tone. "We've known each other less than two weeks, and every minute has been a knife-fight. I need two minutes, Scarlett. Two minutes to acknowledge that we are insane, broken, and completely tethered to each other. I need to know you are still here."

"I'm here, Arthur," she whispered, her hand reaching out to trace the angry cut above his eyebrow. The tenderness felt impossibly fragile against the backdrop of the stolen car and the looming threat. "We survive this, and we start over. I swear it."

He pulled her close, his good arm wrapping fiercely around her. This kiss was different. It wasn't the frantic, animal consumption of the bothy, nor the desperate urgency of the warehouse; it was a vow whispered in the metallic scent of danger and gasoline. It was a promise of a future built on broken foundations. "You're my only objective, Scarlett," he murmured against her mouth.

"Then let's survive this, Arthur," she replied, pulling back, her gaze hard and focused. "Let's ruin him."

▌ The New Target

AJ, moving with the controlled stiffness of a wounded man, grabbed the pistol and checked the car park perimeter. He led them away from the shadows and toward the gleaming, anonymous geometry of the financial district. They moved quickly, blending—or trying to—with the few late-evening workers and residents. The darkness was a necessary mercy.

"The building," AJ said, pointing toward a sleek, anonymous tower of black glass. "It's owned by a firm that matches Gary's known property portfolio—he uses it as a central hub. My contact, Dave, is on the fourth floor."

They bypassed the building's main security, using a rarely used service elevator that smelled faintly of cleaning fluid and damp cardboard. On the fourth floor, the hallway was silent. AJ paused outside a plain steel door marked "Data Recovery." He knocked a specific, complex rhythm—a remnant of their shared military training.

The door opened just a crack. "Dave," AJ whispered, his voice low and urgent. "We need a secure terminal. It's a matter of national security."

Dave, a bald, tired-looking man in a wrinkled t-shirt, assessed the two fugitives—the bruised soldier and the exhausted solicitor—in a single, weary glance. He must have recognized the gravity in AJ's eyes. "You have twenty minutes," he hissed, opening the door wider. "Don't touch the main server. And Arthur, I genuinely don't want to know who you killed this time."

Scarlett moved instantly to the nearest workstation, the lawyer reclaiming her weapon of choice. She barely glanced at the screen before her fingers began flying across the keyboard with startling speed and precision.

AJ watched, surprised by the fluidity of her motions, a skill set he hadn't known she possessed. "You're fast on that thing," he murmured.

Scarlett didn't look up, her eyes glued to the command line. "Boarding school," she replied, the detail dropped casually into the chaos. "They decided all the classic languages—Latin, Greek, French—were useless. They taught us coding instead. All of them. Said it was the only real language of power in the 21st century." She paused, finally meeting his gaze, a slight, grim smile touching her lips. "Never thought I'd use it to track a drug lord's shell corporations."

She turned back to the screen, her focus absolute. "Gary's financial records are my priority," she stated. "I need access to Companies House and the Land Registry. I'm going to follow the money, Arthur. That's the only way we dismantle the bassline."

The city hummed outside the window, unaware that two fugitives—a soldier and a solicitor, strangers who had become essential to one another—were about to launch the decisive battle of their lives from the fourth floor of an office tower.

Chapter 51: The Moment of Stillness

The Vauxhall Corsa shuddered to a final, violent halt in a shadowy, multi-storey car park near the city's financial district. The air was heavy with the smell of stale exhaust and cold concrete. The engine was instantly killed, plunging the small cabin into a tense silence. "Fifteen minutes, maximum," AJ muttered, his voice tight. "The ANPR alert is active. Every patrol car in a three-mile radius is looking for this license plate."

Scarlett was slumped against the passenger door, her mind a cold landscape of loss: no home, no job, no future, and officially branded a murderer on every news channel. The exhaustion was immense, but the adrenaline remained, a thin, painful shield.

AJ didn't immediately move toward the door. He turned to her, his dark eyes intense, searching her face for a sign of collapse. "We just faced down death twice, you watched me set my own bone, and you ran from three armed officers alone," he said, his voice dropping to a low, raw tone. "We've known each other less than two weeks, and every minute has been a knife-fight. I need two minutes, Scarlett. Two minutes to acknowledge that we are insane, broken, and completely tethered to each other. I need to know you are still here."

"I'm here, Arthur," she whispered, her hand reaching out to trace the angry cut above his eyebrow. The tenderness felt impossibly fragile against the backdrop of the stolen car and the looming threat. "We survive this, and we start over. I swear it."

He pulled her close, his good arm wrapping fiercely around her. This kiss was different. It wasn't the frantic, animal consumption of the bothy, nor the desperate urgency of the warehouse; it was a vow whispered in the metallic scent of danger and gasoline. It was a promise of a future built on broken foundations. "You're my only objective, Scarlett," he murmured against her mouth.

"Then let's survive this, Arthur," she replied, pulling back, her gaze hard and focused. "Let's ruin him."

The New Target

AJ, moving with the controlled stiffness of a wounded man, grabbed the pistol and checked the car park perimeter. He led them away from the shadows and toward the gleaming, anonymous geometry of the financial district. They moved quickly, blending—or trying to—with the few late-evening workers and residents. The darkness was a necessary mercy.

"The building," AJ said, pointing toward a sleek, anonymous tower of black glass. "It's owned by a firm that matches Gary's known property portfolio—he uses it as a central hub. My contact, Dave, is on the fourth floor."

They bypassed the building's main security, using a rarely used service elevator that smelled faintly of cleaning fluid and damp cardboard. On the fourth floor, the hallway was silent. AJ paused outside a plain steel door marked "Data Recovery." He knocked a specific, complex rhythm—a remnant of their shared military training.

The door opened just a crack. "Dave," AJ whispered, his voice low and urgent. "We need a secure terminal. It's a matter of national security."

Dave, a bald, tired-looking man in a wrinkled t-shirt, assessed the two fugitives—the bruised soldier and the exhausted solicitor—in a single, weary glance. He must have recognized the gravity in AJ's eyes. "You have twenty minutes," he hissed, opening the door wider. "Don't touch the main server. And Arthur, I genuinely don't want to know who you killed this time."

Scarlett moved instantly to the nearest workstation, the lawyer reclaiming her weapon of choice. She barely glanced at the screen before her fingers began flying across the keyboard with startling speed and precision.

AJ watched, surprised by the fluidity of her motions, a skill set he hadn't known she possessed. "You're fast on that thing," he murmured.

Scarlett didn't look up, her eyes glued to the command line. "Boarding school," she replied, the detail dropped casually into the chaos. "They decided all the classic languages—Latin, Greek, French—were useless. They taught us coding instead. All of them. Said it was the only real language of power in the 21st century." She paused, finally meeting his gaze, a slight, grim smile touching her lips. "Never thought I'd use it to track a drug lord's shell corporations."

She turned back to the screen, her focus absolute. "Gary's financial records are my priority," she stated. "I need access to Companies House and the Land Registry. I'm going to follow the money, Arthur. That's the only way we dismantle the bassline."

The city hummed outside the window, unaware that two fugitives—a soldier and a solicitor, strangers who had become essential to one another—were about to launch the decisive battle of their lives from the fourth floor of an office tower.

Chapter 52: Accessing the Bassline

Scarlett's fingers flew across the keyboard, moving with a blur of efficiency that impressed even AJ. The secure terminal was her battlefield, and she instantly recognized the vulnerabilities of the system before her. She had gained access to the inner network using a common vulnerability: an unsecured administrative login and password she found in an unencrypted client inbox, a glaring security failure on the data recovery firm's network. This single exploit provided her with the crucial bridge to the higher-level financial systems.

"Companies House first," Scarlett instructed, the rhythm of her voice matching the rapid clicks of the keyboard. "We need Gary's full registered details, Arthur. What's his legal identity?"

"Gary Mason," AJ replied, standing guard near the door, his eyes scanning the corridor through the narrow crack. "His formal name is Gareth Mason. DOB: 1960."

The public Companies House database provided the initial identity, but Scarlett immediately went deeper, using her access to bypass the usual paywalls and throttling. "There. The database returns Mason Property Holdings Ltd., registered in the Cayman Islands. A classic offshore shell. The front is a high-volume property firm. They're using it to wash cash and store assets—the volume of transactions is staggering."

She began pulling the detailed corporate filings. "The financial statements—they're obviously inflated. They're using a common technique, overvaluing several industrial properties in the city center to explain massive, untraceable cash deposits."

Scarlett didn't stop. She executed a complex SQL query through a backend port to pull detailed ownership and usage data from the restricted Land Registry data, bypassing the normal public interface. "A series of derelict warehouses near the docks," she confirmed, reading the results scrolling rapidly on her screen. "Registered value is minimal, but they've all had extensive, unlisted structural work—new power lines, reinforced foundations. They're being fortified."

"Secure storage," AJ confirmed instantly, recognizing the tactical implication. "Gary's true safe houses. The operational core—not just for drugs, but possibly for key personnel or captured assets." The gravity of his capture location increased tenfold.

The Paper Trail

Scarlett shifted her focus, executing a sophisticated search across the firm's unencrypted communication logs, hunting for banking details. She found the core accounts and ran an immediate transactional search, requiring a moment of intense coding focus. "There. Two days ago. A single, enormous withdrawal of £500,000, transferred to a private account in Switzerland."

"That's his bolt-hole cash," AJ stated, the realization chilling. "He's planning to disappear. He knew the raid was coming."

"We need to dump this entire file—corporate registration, property plans, and the wire transfer proof—onto Deedee's internal server now," Scarlett instructed, pulling the information into a single, massive compressed file. This was the irrefutable evidence Deedee needed to bypass the local corruption.

AJ pulled a military-grade flash drive from a hidden seam in his tracksuit pocket. Scarlett initiated the massive transfer of data, routing it through multiple proxy layers directly onto Deedee's internal, secure server—a process that would be flagged, but only after the transmission was complete.

"You have ten minutes before I delete your session history," Dave muttered from his workbench, deliberately not looking at the screen, aware of the nature of the transaction.

Scarlett leaned back slightly, her hands trembling from the strain and the psychological pressure. *Fallow Ground may have been a lie, Arthur,* she thought, watching the transfer bar inch forward, *but this is the truth. This is the bassline's end.* The silence in the room was electric, defined only by the quiet hum of the powerful computer and the final ticking of their operational clock.

Chapter 53: The Clock Runs Out

The data transfer progress bar—a thin strip of blue light on the encrypted screen—felt like the slowest thing in the world. It was a digital countdown to freedom, or recapture.

"Five minutes left," Dave muttered, pacing the perimeter of the soundproof office, his anxiety palpable. Sweat beaded on his forehead. "If I get a ping from the central system, I have to wipe everything. Your session goes with it."

Scarlett didn't respond; she was watching the file names flash past: *Mason Properties Cayman Ledger*, *Dockyard Structural Assessment*, *Utility Transfer Logs*. The data represented Gary's operational structure, and she was watching it hemorrhage onto Deedee's secure server.

AJ stood near the door, pistol tucked into his waistband, his posture rigid. He wasn't just guarding; he was watching her work.

I've seen surgeons work under pressure, engineers, pilots... but never like this, AJ thought, watching Scarlett command the terminal. *She's terrifyingly focused. It's the precision of a trained sniper, aimed at a spreadsheet.* He had specialized in recognizing threats and anomalies, but Scarlett was the beautiful anomaly he couldn't have predicted. *She's using a keyboard like it's a weapon, and God help me, I'm completely in awe.*

"We need to assume Gary's mole, Drayton, had a remote alert built into Deedee's system," AJ said, his voice low. "If Deedee accesses this data, Drayton gets flagged. That's our maximum safe window. The transfer has to finish before the internal sweep moves from investigation to containment."

Dave, glancing over at Scarlett's intense, focused profile, leaned in toward AJ and whispered, keeping his voice low enough not to disturb her concentration. "Flick of the wrist, eh? Mate, watching her work the keyboard... there's something seriously sexy about a bird who can hack the Land Registry like that. Gets the blood going, doesn't it, squaddy?"

AJ's jaw tightened, not in agreement, but in raw, possessive acknowledgement of the observation. He just grunted a noncommittal response, his attention snapping back to the threat.

"Three minutes!" Dave called out, checking his wrist. "My internal timer just hit red!"

The Final Intel

Scarlett leaned closer to the monitor. Her focus wasn't just on the transfer; it was on the Land Registry database she still had open. She was running one last, desperate query—cross-referencing the structural work against the municipal permits.

"Arthur, look at this," she instructed, her voice urgent. "The structural work on the dockyard warehouses—it wasn't just reinforcement. There's a mention of an unlisted sub-level facility added last year. Heavy load-bearing columns. Too much for drug storage."

"It's a detention and interrogation unit," AJ confirmed grimly, his face hardening as he processed the potential horror. "This is where he's keeping assets—or people. This is where they would take me."

The file transfer hit 98%.

"Time's up!" Dave yelled, rushing the desk, his voice cracking. "I'm wiping the session! Now!"

Scarlett ignored him, her fingers flying one last time. She quickly printed the specific sub-level schematic to a small, isolated printer Dave kept in the corner. The image was grainy, black-and-white, but horrifyingly clear: two interconnected cells and a central access shaft.

"Done!" she shouted, tearing the paper from the machine just as Dave slammed his hand down on the keyboard, executing the wipe command. The screens instantly went black.

Exit Strategy

The sudden darkness was broken by a sound that made AJ freeze, instantly overriding the adrenaline: the rhythmic, high-pitched ping of a police radio clicking to life, audible from the stairwell outside the steel door.

"They're here," AJ said, grabbing Scarlett's hand. "The local precinct. Gary got the ANPR alert, and he didn't wait for the internal mole. He's deploying his corrupt assets to the car park."

"The ventilation shaft!" Scarlett yelled, shoving the schematic printout into the neck of her hoodie.

AJ pulled her out of the office and into the emergency stairwell, moving upward with shocking speed despite his injury. They reached the rooftop access door. "We go over," AJ commanded, pulling the thick rope they'd carried from the bothy. He secured the rope around a solid ventilation unit. "I go first. I secure the drop, and you follow. This is the last leap, lawyer."

"Go, Arthur."

Chapter 54: The Drop and the Getaway

The air on the skyscraper rooftop was cold, sharp, and carried the metallic stench of the city. Below them lay the concrete canyon of the financial district. AJ didn't hesitate. He pulled Scarlett tight against his side and kissed her briefly on the forehead, a final, fierce confirmation of their bond.

He went over the parapet first, his taped left arm useless, relying entirely on the powerful muscles of his right shoulder and core to control the descent. The hemp rope—the same rope used to secure the hatch—burned through his gloved hand. He braced his feet against the sheer glass wall of the adjacent, slightly lower building, slowing his rapid slide.

AJ stopped their slide abruptly, planting his feet firmly against the glass wall. "Your turn, lawyer! Over the edge now!" he shouted, his voice echoing down to the roof they had just left. He needed her on the rope so he could control both their weights simultaneously.

Scarlett forced herself to move, fighting the inertia and the sheer terror of the height. She pushed herself over the edge, let go, and felt the sudden, agonizing jerk as his right arm took her weight, controlling the speed of her fall by tightening the rope. The friction was immense, and she could smell the burnt hemp.

They descended the four-story gap silently, the rough rope tearing at the fabric of her borrowed clothes, finally landing lightly on the roof of the slightly lower adjacent tower. AJ released the rope, letting it coil onto the roof, and collapsed instantly onto the gravelled surface.

"I need five seconds," he gasped, his chest heaving, his face slick with sweat and pain. His right arm, their only functional limb, was shaking violently.

"No time, Arthur," she said, already pulling the schematic of the sub-level facility from her hoodie. "They know we're here. We need to go down. The sub-level access is key—if they're using the docks, they need proximity to major transport lines. We hit the docks now."

The Final Descent

They began a rapid, brutal descent through the building's exterior fire escape, the cold metal railing biting into their hands. The alarm system on the office tower remained silent—a testament to Dave's effective security lockdown.

They hit the ground floor of a narrow, debris-strewn service alley. The immediate noise of the city—traffic, sirens, distant shouts—felt overwhelming after the silence of the moors and the office tower. AJ pulled Scarlett into the deep shadow of a steel dumpster just as the first local police car—a heavy, black and white van—screeched around the corner, its blue lights flashing but its siren blissfully silent, operating in search mode.

AJ didn't flinch. He recognized the tactical threat instantly: corrupt local officers executing Gary's immediate recapture order based on the ANPR ping.

He emerged from the shadows just as the officer rounded the corner of the van, pistol already drawn and aiming for center mass. "Stop! Police! Show me your hands!" the officer barked, his voice tense but steady.

"Corrupt police," AJ muttered, his eyes cold and assessing. He raised his taped, mangled left shoulder—a feint—drawing the officer's aim slightly high. AJ lunged, using the pistol not as a firearm, but as a blunt striking tool, slamming the heavy weapon into the officer's face with brutal efficiency. The officer dropped instantly, the impact snapping his head back against the van door.

Assaulting the Bassline

AJ grabbed the keys, which were dangling from the officer's belt, and jumped into the idling police van. The interior smelled of stale coffee and cheap plastic. He slammed on the brakes, the sudden stop jolting Scarlett forward.

"Get in!" he roared, his voice laced with renewed urgency and adrenaline.

Scarlett scrambled inside, throwing herself onto the passenger seat just as the police van shot out of the alley and onto the main road. The irony was devastating: they were now driving a stolen police vehicle—an official symbol of authority—through the heart of Manchester, directly toward Gary's dockyard stronghold.

AJ glanced at her, the blue lights strobing across his bruised face. The vehicle was conspicuous, but also granted them immediate tactical advantage. "We're no longer running," he stated, his voice a low, fierce promise. "We're assaulting the bassline."

Chapter 55: The Stolen Sanctuary

The stolen police van—a massive, throbbing target—screamed through the Manchester streets. The vehicle was a temporary paradox: a shield of authority granting immediate right-of-way, but a ticking time bomb visible on every ANPR camera. AJ drove with ruthless, focused speed, his knuckles white on the wheel. Scarlett, slumped in the passenger seat, was trying to use the stolen police radio to track local police movements, but the static was overwhelming, broken only by garbled, fast-spoken alerts that offered no clear intelligence.

AJ reached down and ripped the microphone cable free from the console, simultaneously smashing the integrated GPS unit with the pistol grip. The plastic shattered violently.

"Their active track on this vehicle is dead now," he grated, his voice tight. "We have about ten minutes before they switch to ANPR search grids. We need to be invisible before then."

"We can't take this to the docks," AJ confirmed, turning the van sharply off the main road. "It's too visible. We need a moment to breathe, clean the wounds, and recover from the shock and pain. You need time to shake off the last of that chemical fog before we hit Gary's fortress."

He pulled the van into the vast, echoing shadow of a derelict Victorian warehouse, cutting the engine instantly. The silence was immediate and profound, broken only by their ragged breathing and the faint tick of the cooling metal.

Pressure Release

Scarlett leaned across the console, her eyes dark and burning. "Well, this is one way to violate police property," she whispered, the absurd statement a direct acknowledgment of their profound, terrifying situation.

AJ didn't hesitate. He pulled her across the console, hauling her into the rear of the van, where the uncomfortable metal seating and cold vinyl walls offered no comfort.

He pressed her body against the cold, hard seats, desperation in his touch. There was no gentleness; this was pure, ragged urgency driven by the brutal knowledge they were likely going to die today. His good arm anchored her, the other hand working with swift, functional efficiency, pulling away the layers of borrowed clothes. He moved immediately, pulling them together, their bodies colliding with the raw, consuming force of two people fighting back against oblivion.

A sharp, breathless sound tore from her throat—a mixture of pain and profound, desperate pleasure. She braced her hands desperately against the dashboard, her fingers digging into the hard plastic, matching his animalistic rhythm. The intensity was overwhelming, pushing her to the brink of release.

"Arthur!" she gasped, the name a plea and a final surrender as her body dissolved into a rush of chaotic feeling.

Her release was enough to shatter his remaining control. With a final, ragged thrust, he collapsed onto her back, panting and slick with sweat, his entire weight grounding her to the present. They lay there, two broken fugitives clinging to the physical reality of their survival, the silence of the van heavy with the shared necessity of the moment.

"We have twenty minutes," he stated, his voice instantly returning to the professional tone. "We need to plan our entry."

Phase I: Tactical Assessment

Scarlett began meticulously searching the storage compartments and the back cabinet of the police van, forcing her focus onto immediate, practical assets. This was the most effective part of their time.

- Weapons: "We have three additional magazines for the pistol. Full load. Total rounds: thirty-nine. And two sets of standard police cuffs."
- Tools: "A crowbar, a heavy-duty bolt cutter, a small battery-powered angle grinder, and several lengths of rope and chain. They use this van for lockups and structural access."
- Comms: "The main radio is useless—it's tracked and compromised. We ditch the handset, but keep the charger for the burner phone."

"The bolt cutter and the angle grinder are our entry tools," AJ confirmed, reviewing the arsenal. "The detention unit is sub-level, reinforced steel. We can't blow the door, but we can cut the hinges and the locks."

"If we cut the power and comms before we enter, we buy a window," Scarlett mused, analyzing the facility's likely weaknesses.

AJ nodded, his plan forming. "We go in silent, eliminate the perimeter, cut the power, and then we hit the sub-level hinges. Our only goal is to find the detention unit and retrieve any evidence we can use to secure my release and your name."

Chapter 56: The Utility Cut

AJ and Scarlett suited up in the back of the stolen police van. The shift in clothing was immediate and profound. AJ donned a high-visibility vest that was several sizes too large, the bright orange a cynical piece of camouflage. Scarlett did the same, pulling her hair back tight and zipping the vest over her dark hoodie.

Scarlett adjusted her own hi-vis vest, looking down at the borrowed trousers and the oversized top underneath. "You know," she mused, a wry smile touching her lips, "in the last two weeks, I've gone from a raving drug moll to Vincent Vega in borrowed clothes, and now, apparently, a municipal supervisor. I've had more costume changes than the Village People."

"I'm a contracted electrical supervisor," AJ stated, ignoring the joke, but a muscle twitched in his jaw. "You are my apprentice. You look scared, but that's normal for an apprentice who just got yelled at."

They located the utility bank quickly, a large, exposed junction box tucked behind a rusted service access gate on the side of the dockyard warehouse. AJ moved with agonizing care, his one good arm taking all the strain. He grabbed the heavy-duty bolt cutter and the battery-powered angle grinder from the supplies they had organized, the metal tools clanking softly.

He didn't speak. He went straight for the communications line first. He positioned the heavy-duty bolt cutter around the thick comms cable—the primary fiber link for the entire complex. With a clean, sharp SNAP that sliced through the night air, the cable was instantly severed, cutting off all external communication and internal security monitoring systems reliant on that fiber link.

The Blind Flash

"Arthur, wait," Scarlett called out, her voice tight, pulling him back into the shadows of the service gate. "The gate. Two local patrol cars are pulling up."

The sight of the black and white police vans was chilling. They weren't moving fast; they were simply taking up defensive positions at the main entrance and the secondary vehicle gate. "They're not looking for us; they're protecting the building," AJ grated, understanding the tactical reality. "Gary knows we hit his finances. He's expecting an official raid, not a two-person insertion team."

AJ knew he couldn't wait for them to finish positioning. He flicked the switch on the angle grinder. The motor screamed to life, a high, piercing whine that momentarily covered the sound of the approaching officers. He positioned himself over the power line—a thick, armored industrial cable adjacent to the severed comms link.

He drove the whirring blade hard into the thick, armored power cable.

The scream of the grinder was instantly replaced by a brilliant, blinding blue flash and a deafening CRACK that echoed across the docks. The sheer force of the short-circuit threw AJ back against the stone wall, the electrical discharge briefly illuminating his grim, shocked face. The entire complex was instantly plunged into absolute, suffocating darkness, the transition from industrial light and operational buzz to pitch black complete and sudden.

Confusion was immediate. They heard sharp shouts, the immediate blast of a police siren (the wrong response, indicating panic), and the frustrated crackle of police radios—now useless without external comms.

"Go! Go! Go!" AJ yelled, dropping the now-useless, sparking grinder and grabbing the heavy crowbar—a formidable weapon of last resort. He was breathing hard, the shock of the electrical discharge and the exertion adding to the agonizing pain in his shoulder.

Insertion

They melted into the chaotic darkness. The air was thick with the smell of ozone and burnt plastic. AJ moved with a renewed, desperate speed, pulling Scarlett along the side of the warehouse, away from the confused officers fumbling with flashlights and communication issues near the entrance.

"The side door!" AJ whispered, pointing to a service entrance marked by a rusted metal fire escape. "They won't secure the perimeter until the main power is restored."

They reached the door. AJ used the crowbar, twisting the metal with controlled, single-armed effort. The lock mechanism shrieked, then gave way with a final, tearing snap. They slipped inside, leaving the chaos of the police vans and the dark dockyard behind them.

The window was open. The target was blind.

Scarlett leaned against the cold interior wall, pulling the hi-vis vest tighter around her. "Just focus on the current costume, lawyer. We're still on the clock."

Chapter 57: Perimeter Breach

AJ and Scarlett moved quickly along the side of the vast, dark warehouse toward the main perimeter fence, using the heavy crowbar AJ carried as a necessary, cumbersome grounding point. The silence following the power cut was now their chief weapon, broken only by the sporadic, muffled shouts of the confused local police officers near the main gate. The entire compound smelled of brine, rust, and the faint, burnt plastic residue from the angle grinder.

"The gate," AJ muttered, his voice tight. "It's electronic. The power's out, so the lock should be dead."

"We need a moment, Arthur," Scarlett whispered, scanning the area. The officers were too close to the fence line. "We need to pull them away from the breach point."

"Distraction," AJ agreed, instantly understanding her intent. He hurled a heavy chunk of broken concrete he'd found toward a nearby stack of empty wooden pallets. The resulting CLATTER and crash of splintering wood was loud enough to sound like a major structural failure. The corrupt officers, already operating on high alert in the pitch black, reacted instantly, their flashlights whipping erratically as they sprinted toward the source of the noise.

AJ shoved the massive steel security gate open, relying purely on his remaining strength now that the electronic lock was dead. They slipped inside the perimeter, moving from the darkness of the exterior into the deeper, suffocating darkness of the warehouse grounds.

Infiltration Tools

They bypassed the main, high-traffic doors, heading instead toward a small, reinforced loading bay door at the back—the least conspicuous point of entry. "Hinges," AJ reminded her. "We use the cutter first."

He positioned the heavy-duty bolt cutter against the reinforced steel of the top hinge. The effort was immense, requiring his full body weight and his good arm straining against the leverage. With a groan of tortured metal and a loud CLANG, the top hinge snapped. Scarlett quickly handed him the crowbar. He used the crowbar to pry the door outward, forcing the bottom hinge to sheer under the pressure.

AJ pushed the door inward with a sharp kick, revealing a cold, echoing warehouse interior smelling of brine and rust. "Detention unit access is through a service stairwell below the administration office," AJ breathed, pointing to a dark, narrow opening across the floor. "This is Gary's heart—the true center of his operation."

They navigated the cavernous, pitch-black space, moving silently across the slick concrete floor, careful to avoid tripping over unseen equipment. They finally reached a heavily reinforced door at the bottom of the service stairs. It was secured not by a modern electronic lock, but by a massive, old-fashioned padlock and chain—a redundant, low-tech security measure, put there for show and to deter common thieves.

The Final Show

AJ paused, his hand gripping the cold steel of the padlock. He noticed the thin, almost imperceptible gap beneath the door. He knelt, his eyes adjusting to the darkness, and saw a faint, consistent line of light emanating from the sub-level. "There's light," he whispered. "Gary is still down there. He's waiting for us."

AJ stood up, his gaze sweeping the space. He lifted the heavy, stolen bolt cutter—a massive, cumbersome tool—and deliberately brought it down not on the chain, but smashed it with thunderous force against the concrete wall adjacent to the door. The sound was a clear, deliberate CLANG that echoed through the entire silent building, announcing their arrival like a thunderclap.

"Surprise is overrated," AJ hissed, dropping the cutter and reaching for the crowbar. He looked at Scarlett, a cold, intense fire in his eyes. "Let's give him a show. We eliminate the advantage of stealth and take the advantage of shock."

The door was silent, but the challenge had been issued. Gary knew they were coming. The final confrontation was now minutes, not hours, away.

Chapter 58: The Retrieval

The resounding CLANG of the bolt cutter against the concrete wall—AJ's deliberate challenge—echoed violently down the service stairs. "They're down here! Get them!" Gary's voice screamed from beyond the steel door, laced with fury and anticipation.

AJ grabbed the stolen pistol, but retreated suddenly, dragging Scarlett back up the steps and into the deeper darkness of the warehouse interior. "Bait," AJ explained, his breath ragged. "I can't waste ammo on a door. They want me alive. We create chaos and draw them out."

He knew exactly where Gary would appear. He pushed Scarlett behind a stack of empty crates near the administration office stairwell. Gary, followed by a single, uniformed guard, burst onto the main warehouse floor, flashlights cutting uselessly through the absolute darkness.

AJ immediately opened fire, aiming three calculated shots at the concrete wall just behind Gary. The bullets ricocheted with a whining *PING*, creating noise and psychological pressure. Scarlett, without instruction, understood the chaos strategy. She tossed the heavy rope they'd carried low across the floor, stretching it taught between two support beams—a perfect, low-tech tripwire.

The guard hit the tripwire instantly, collapsing forward with a crash of plastic and equipment. "Go! Run! Through the loading bay!" AJ yelled, firing a final shot to keep Gary pinned down.

The Real Target

She was halfway across the vast warehouse floor, sprinting toward the heavy, reinforced loading bay door (their initial breach point), when she was tackled hard and brutally from the side. The impact sent a fresh wave of agony through her stitched ribs.

"Not so fast, lawyer!" Michael's voice—rough, vengeful, and unmistakable—snarled in her ear. The blow to his skull from the steel chair had clearly not been fatal. Michael, the thug AJ had knocked out at the interrogation cell, was back, moving with frightening speed.

She was pinned instantly. Michael slammed her against the concrete floor, his massive hand instantly clamping around her throat, cutting off her airway. Scarlett clawed at his fingers like a wild animal, thrashing and choking, panic flooding her system as his weight pinned her down, leveraging the ground for instant compliance.

"Look, copper! The merchandise is secured!" Michael yelled toward the distant sounds of AJ's diversionary shots. "She's ours now! Go!" Michael screamed, dragging Scarlett backwards toward the newly breached service stairs.

AJ saw Michael capture Scarlett, and the truth hit him with sickening force: Gary hadn't wanted him. Gary wanted the analyst—the lawyer who had effortlessly hacked his entire financial front and was now an unpredictable threat. The capture was revenge, psychological torture, and business all at once. The thought of her being trafficked—the "product"—while AJ was forced to live with the knowledge shattered him.

AJ's tactical mind fought his survival instinct. He fired three rapid suppression rounds toward Gary and the guard, forcing them to duck and momentarily halting their pursuit. He used the crucial second of cover not to charge Michael, but to escape, sprinting toward the deepest shadows near the loading bay. He was forced to make the agonizing tactical retreat: save himself to save her later. He disappeared into the darkness, leaving Scarlett screaming his name.

The Holding

Scarlett was dragged through the access panel and down into the sub-level service stairwell, the air instantly colder and heavier. Michael was panting, his grip bruising her arm. He didn't take her to the main room; he dragged her toward a small, lateral, reinforced door she hadn't seen on the schematic.

He shoved her inside a small, dark cell that smelled faintly of brine and sweat. "Gary said you're high value. We're keeping you safe... for testing. Arthur can play his hero games all night. You're our bait now."

He slammed the steel door shut. The heavy bolt slid into place with a deafening, final *CLACK*.

Scarlett stood trembling in the absolute darkness. The knowledge of her impending fate, the pain, the betrayal, and the sheer terror of Michael's face overwhelmed her. She was captive again. And AJ was gone, forced to abandon her for the second time, this time knowing exactly what awaited her.

Chapter 59: The Counter-Assault

The next day felt like an eternity compressed into a few minutes of dawn. Scarlett was still in the sub-level cell. The long hours had been punctuated by brutal, non-stop interrogations carried out by Michael and his men. She was cold, exhausted, and the psychological trauma and near-starvation made her attempts to think clearly agonizing. Every movement sent a fresh spike of pain through her ribs and thighs, evidence of the rough, calculated beating she had endured—designed to break her spirit and her knowledge.

The greatest anguish, however, was the profound violation that went beyond the blows; her mind flicked back to the hands all over her, the suffocating presence of their captors, and the cold, internal dread that had ripped through her when they realized she was completely helpless. Her laying pinned to the floor sobbing whilst they inflicted something worse than pain—a calculated, degrading abuse designed to break her mentally. Yet, even facing that absolute violation, her spirit held. She didn't break.

They had demanded to know what AJ knew, what Deedee knew, and how a solicitor accessed the financial records. Scarlett had given them nothing but defiance. During the worst of the abuse, when the cold, focused blows were relentless, she found a strange, resilient anchor:

"So give me all your poison / And give me all your pills / And give me all your hopeless hearts / And make me ill," she'd recited, her voice a cracked, defiant whisper, forcing the words out even as Michael snarled in frustrated rage and contempt. "You're running after something / That you'll never kill / If this is what you want / Then fire at will." The lyric was an aggressive, perfect summary of her refusal to yield.

When they had finally left her alone again, she was dumped unceremoniously on the cold, bloodied and ruined concrete floor of her cell. Her body ached with deep, debilitating fatigue, but her mind, though hazy with pain, refused to break. To defy them in the agonizing silence, to assert her broken will, she began to sing, a low, tuneless drone that was meant for no one but herself, yet still carried in the confined space. "...Exit light. Enter night. Take my hand. Off to never-never land," she croaked, a distorted, off-key rendition of the lyric, her voice cracking more and more with each new wave of pain. The words were a plea for release and a commitment to the fight.

The occasional guard passing by would slam a fist against her bars. "Shut your bloody trap, slag!" they'd yell. But Scarlett just kept singing, a broken record of defiance. It was a small, pathetic act, but it was fiercely hers.

The Tactical Retaliation

Then, she heard it: not the thumping of machinery, but the sudden, urgent shatter of glass followed by a distinctive series of rapid, muffled gunshots from the processing floor above. Arthur.

A wave of overwhelming relief and terror washed over her. He hadn't abandoned her. He had gone for backup.

The sounds of a full-scale firefight erupted, closer and brutally professional. The air in the sub-level detention unit vibrated with the heavy, controlled roar of automatic weapons fire—not the sloppy exchange of pistols, but sustained, tactical engagement. This was a dedicated assault unit. A voice, clear and cold, cut through the noise: "Deedee! Move to the secondary control!" Arthur had come back, and he hadn't come back alone.

The light in the corridor outside her cell flickered violently and then went out entirely, plunged into absolute darkness by a secondary power cut, broken only by the sporadic muzzle flashes filtering through the main access panel.

The heavy steel door to the detention unit was suddenly ripped inward with a deafening screech—cut through by the very angle grinder AJ had abandoned, now wielded by a professional. AJ stood in the doorway, his face blackened with soot and focus, his sidearm smoking. He was flanked by two other figures in black tactical gear—AFOs from Deedee's unit.

"Scarlett! I'm here!" AJ roared, his voice thick with raw emotion and adrenaline. He rushed to the cell door, firing two precise, rapid shots that shredded the lock mechanism.

"Arthur!" Scarlett stumbled out, her body bruised and shaking, running toward the only light and safety she knew. The reunion was immediate and chaotic. AJ grabbed her, pulling her against his body in a fierce, desperate hug, his good arm a steel band around her waist.

The Final Shot

But the battle wasn't over. Gary, cunning and calculating, had anticipated the immediate counter-assault and the need to destroy the primary witness. From the shadows of the adjacent cell block, a figure lunged. It wasn't a guard; it was Gary, dressed in black tactical gear, holding a powerful, suppressed rifle.

"You lose, copper!" Gary screamed, his face contorted in final rage, firing one single, controlled shot aimed directly at AJ's chest. AJ saw the flash, his body reacting instantly, the ingrained instinct overriding all pain. He shoved Scarlett hard behind him, his own body vaulting into the air to take the impact. The bullet missed AJ, passing through the space he had just occupied.

Scarlett felt a burning, agonizing sledgehammer strike her in the side—the stray round tearing through her body. She gasped, the pain absolute and consuming. Her legs instantly gave out. She heard AJ's guttural scream—a sound of pure, immediate devastation.

Before she hit the ground, AJ unleashed a savage, continuous spray of bullets into Gary's position. The tactical unit behind him immediately returned fire, turning the corridor into a maelstrom of violent light and noise. Gary screamed—a sound of pure rage and sudden injury—as he was hit and fell.

Scarlett was deafened, her side a pooling abyss of heat and agony. Her vision swam, filling with the sudden, overwhelming scarlet red of blood. The last sensation Scarlett registered, before the pain and the darkness took over, was the overwhelming, desperate strength of Arthur's arms lifting her, pulling her against his shoulder. He moved with the brutal, single-minded focus of an officer carrying a fallen comrade. She was held tightly, her body limp and broken, but eternally safe in the embrace of the man who had lost everything for her. He was running, carrying her out of the blood-soaked ruin of the bassline. She looked up, just for a moment, and saw the raw, unshed tears streaming down his soot-blackened face.

Chapter 60: The Silent Scream

The world outside the sub-level detention unit was a maelstrom of gunfire, shouting, and flashing red and blue lights. Arthur ran, oblivious to the remaining firefight, carrying Scarlett's limp, bleeding body. The immediate, searing heat of her blood soaking into his jacket was the only reality he registered.

He slid down a concrete corridor, away from the intense center of the fight, laying Scarlett gently against a cold, relatively dry wall. He tore the hi-vis vest from his own body and jammed the thick fabric hard against the spreading wound in her flank.

"Stay with me, Scarlett, stay with me!" Arthur pleaded, his voice a hoarse, ragged sound of raw desperation. He pressed down with all his remaining strength, leveraging his good arm against the injury. He could feel the weakness in her breathing. "Look at me! Look at me, lawyer! You are not done! You don't get to quit now! You hear me? We have a life to start! Don't you dare close your eyes!" He repeated the words like a litany, trying to anchor her consciousness to his voice, his heat, the pressure of his hand.

Finally, two minutes later, tactical medics—AFOs who were now doubling as emergency personnel—reached them. Arthur only released her, his hands shaking violently, when he knew professionals had taken over. "She took a round, Dee," Arthur rasped to Detective Inspector Hayes, who arrived seconds later, organizing the site. "She took the round that was meant for me. Get her out. Now."

Deedee quickly assessed the scene and the urgency of Scarlett's condition. "We found Michael. He's finished. Gary's gone."

Arthur froze. "Gone? How the fuck is he gone? I saw him fall!"

"We don't know yet. He must have used a secondary escape route after you hit him. He's wounded, but he's gone." Deedee's voice hardened. "Code Black. Direct route to the specialized trauma center. No police contact. We are maintaining the secrecy of this operation."

Arthur felt the physical structure of his exhaustion collapse. He slumped against a cold, metal container, allowing the full weight of his pain and failure to hit him.

The Hospital Debrief

He woke hours later in a secure, silent wing of a private hospital. His shoulder was professionally set, his wounds cleaned and bandaged, and he was heavily medicated against the trauma he had endured. Deedee sat beside his bed, a sterile, unreadable presence in the clean room.

"The network is collapsing," Deedee confirmed, her voice low. "The financial records you secured bought us everything. You're a hero, Arthur. Drayton is talking. You're clear of all charges, and your career is secure. You'll be on desk duty for a long time."

Arthur didn't look at her, the job the furthest thing from his mind. "Scarlett."

"She's stable. Critical, but stable. The round caught her in the flank, missing the major organs. She's in surgery, then a medically induced coma to manage the systemic shock and recovery."

"I failed her, Dee. I was too slow."

"You saved her life, Arthur. But you need to know everything." Deedee's professional composure cracked, replaced by a grim, cold fury. "During stabilization, they ran a full trauma assessment. They found multiple injuries consistent with repeated use of a baton and blunt force. And they confirmed evidence of sustained sexual assault during her detention. They violated her, Arthur. That's why she was broken."

The Last Secret

Deedee pulled out a clean, sealed envelope, her expression now one of profound caution. "Arthur. This is the second part of the trauma blood work. The results came back." Deedee hesitated for a long, heavy moment. "The lab confirmed the presence of hCG—human Chorionic Gonadotropin. She might be pregnant."

Arthur froze, the word "pregnant" echoing in the clean, silent room. "What?"

His mind immediately flashed back to the unspeakable violation she had suffered in the cell, the trauma Michael and Gary inflicted. "Is it... is it from them?" he rasped, the question tearing at his throat, the absolute worst possibility dominating his mind.

Deedee reached out and placed a hand firmly on his arm, her expression softening with quick, professional reassurance. "No, Arthur. The assault happened hours ago. Medically, the timing of conception is consistent with four to five weeks gestation—it couldn't be."

Arthur let out a shuddering breath of profound relief, but his mind was still wrestling with the clinical timeline. "Four to five weeks gestational? That's still too long for our contact. Are you sure, Dee?"

Deedee leaned closer, clarifying the medical distinction. "It's medically confirmed, Arthur. The levels are concerningly low, consistent with four to five weeks gestational age. That timeframe is always calculated from the first day of the last menstrual period, but the actual conceptual age—when fertilization occurred—is two to three weeks ago. It dates back precisely to the beginning of your contact with her."

Arthur absorbed the clinical details, and the relief solidified into fierce certainty. "Then it is mine," he stated, his voice thick with emotion and possessiveness.

"The physical trauma, the stress, and the Rophynol exposure in the weeks leading up to the incident make the situation extremely high-risk. We don't know the extent of the damage, but they are monitoring her levels daily. If they double as expected, they will proceed with a full viability scan."

The revelation of the life they had unknowingly conceived—a life created in the eye of the storm, amidst the chaotic backdrop of stolen cars, violence, and lies—hit Arthur with the force of another physical blow. He was supposed to be a ghost, a solitary operative whose life ended in the shadows. Now, he was potentially a father.

"Four to five weeks gestational," he whispered, absorbing the clinical details. "dating back to our first week." He pulled a shaky breath from his chest. "I need to see her."

Chapter 61: The Vigil

Arthur moved through the sterile white corridors of the secure hospital wing. He was no longer Detective Sergeant Jacobs, nor was he the operative known as Arthur. He was Arthur, the father of a hope that was now precisely four to five weeks gestational age and hanging by a fragile thread. His job, his career, the entire world outside the glass, felt irrelevant.

Scarlett was motionless in the bed, a still, pale figure dominated by the tubes, wires, and monitoring equipment that kept her alive. The steady *beep-beep-beep* of the machines confirmed the continuation of her life, and, impossibly, the life of their child. Her wounds were clean, her bruises fading, but the psychological trauma was a visible stillness beneath the sheet.

Arthur walked to the bedside, his shoulder aching—a dull, constant reminder of the violence he hadn't fully stopped. "I'm sorry," he whispered, resting his hand lightly near her temple. "I'm so sorry, Scarlett. I should have taken the shot myself."

The Agonizing Wait

The next few weeks became an agonizing, desperate loop. Arthur refused to leave her side, establishing a permanent, silent vigil. He watched the sun rise and set over the city, now quietly and systematically pulling apart Gary's organization based on the intelligence Scarlett had salvaged. Deedee reported daily: the property firm was frozen, Drayton was providing details, and the drug processing plant was seized. The bassline was officially silenced.

Every morning, the same trauma doctor came in to deliver the latest hCG results. Day after day, Arthur held his breath. The doubling was slow, cautious, but miraculously, it was happening. The child was fighting the residual trauma and the chemical poison.

The hospital wing became his world. He spoke to her constantly about mundane things—the reports Deedee sent him, the structural damage of the dockyard, and, always, about Jonesy, who was now living a life of spoiled luxury in Deedee's quiet country flat. "I miss the chaos, too, Scarlett. I miss the sound of you arguing legal points while driving a stolen van." He spoke of the life she deserved, the safe, simple life he had risked everything for.

The vigil stretched into weeks. Christmas passed in a blur of antiseptic and silence; the hospital staff decorated the main hall, but the festive cheer felt utterly distant, marking time in the most stark, clinical fashion. Twenty-one days. Twenty-two. Twenty-three. Three weeks after the counter-assault, Scarlett remained in her induced coma.

The First Sign of Return

On a cold Tuesday morning, almost three weeks after the operation and deep into the New Year, Arthur was reading a report detailing the confiscation of Gary's property firm. He was slumped in his chair, lost in the technical jargon, when he felt a faint, slight pressure against his hand, which rested near hers on the sheet. Scarlett's fingers had just tightened.

Arthur's heart slammed into his ribs, instantly overriding the medication and the fatigue. "Scarlett?" he whispered, leaning closer, terrified that the slight movement was simply a reflexive twitch.

Her eyes, which had been closed for what felt like an eternity, finally fluttered open, finding his face through the low light of the bedside lamp. Her focus was slow, but undeniable.

"Arthur?" she rasped, her voice thin and dry from disuse. Her eyes immediately registered the clean sheets, the hospital gown, and the safe, familiar face above her. She managed a single, profound question, the mission the last piece of consciousness she held: "The bassline... did we...?"

Arthur closed his eyes, a wave of profound, agonizing relief washing over him. The lawyer was back. The woman he loved was back. "Yes," he murmured, clutching her hand, resting his forehead on the sheet. "We silenced the bassline. We won, Scarlett. We won."

Chapter 62: The Awakenings (Revised for Timeline)

Arthur gripped Scarlett's hand, the feel of her returned pressure a profound, dizzying relief. "The bassline," he repeated, his voice thick with emotion. "We won, Scarlett. It's over. Gary is gone."

She managed a fragile smile, the sheer effort evident in the tightness around her eyes. "What... what happened?" she whispered, her voice dry and unused.

"You took a bullet," Arthur explained, keeping his voice steady and clinical to avoid alarming her. "A stray round caught you in the flank. You've been resting for three weeks. Medically induced coma, to manage the systemic shock." He carefully relayed the good news. "The network is dismantled. Drayton is talking. Your intelligence won the war. Deedee and her unit are handling the clean-up."

A shadow fell across the room as the trauma doctor entered, a woman in specialized scrubs, her expression professionally cautious. "Welcome back, Ms. Harper," the doctor said softly, approaching the bedside. "Your recovery is crucial now. We need to run some immediate checks—neurological and systemic."

The doctor efficiently checked the vitals and spoke with the nurses, ensuring Scarlett was lucid and stable after the withdrawal of sedation. The assessment was rigorous, lasting nearly ten minutes, leaving Scarlett exhausted but functional.

Once the doctor was satisfied, she dismissed the nurses and addressed Scarlett with extreme gentleness. "Ms. Harper, during the trauma stabilization, we ran a full panel of tests. Because of the nature of your injury and the chemicals found in your system, we need to bring in a specialist for further monitoring."

Scarlett frowned, confused by the medical detour. "Monitoring for what?"

The doctor gently squeezed her hand, offering a look of deep compassion. "I'll let Arthur explain the details, but we need to prioritize a very specific viability test immediately. We will return shortly." The doctor then left, giving them privacy.

The Impossible Truth

Arthur took a deep breath, knowing this was the hardest operational briefing he would ever give. He walked back to the bedside, resting his weight against the mattress, his gaze seeking hers.

"Scarlett, the specialist they mentioned... it's because of the test results," Arthur said, his voice low and firm, bracing himself for her reaction. "When they stabilized you, they found you're pregnant. You're about seven to eight weeks along now."

He felt the immediate need to provide the context that was both the source of their joy and their terror. "It happened just before the raids. It's early, and because of the physical trauma, the surgical intervention, and the residual chemical exposure... it's classified as extremely high-risk."

Scarlett stared at him, the pale features of her face shifting through disbelief, horror, and sudden, piercing understanding. The memory of their raw, urgent passion in the stolen van, the desperate comfort of the bothy, and the chaos of the kitchen—it all clicked into horrifying, beautiful place. "No, Arthur. I can't. Not now.

Not like this. Not after everything. What if it's damaged? What if it's not viable?"

Tears finally welled in her eyes, not of grief, but of profound, overwhelming uncertainty. She looked at the tubes, the scars, and the evidence of the brutality she had endured. "This shouldn't be happening, Arthur. Not to this child."

Arthur pulled her hand gently to his lips, his rough skin brushing her knuckles. "I know this is impossible. This is your body, your life, and your choice. Whatever you decide, I promise you, I will stand by it. I will support your decision completely, no matter how difficult." He looked her straight in the eye, his deep brown gaze unwavering. "If you decide to keep the child, I will dedicate every second of my life to being the father it needs. This is your control, Scarlett. Your terms. Not mine."

The Viability Scan

The sincerity of his promise, the complete surrender of control to her, seemed to calm the frantic terror in her mind. She took a long, shaking breath, accepting the reality. She looked from the empty doorway where the doctor had been to Arthur's resolute face. She lifted her chin slightly, the innate defiance that had powered her through the interrogation returning.

"A scan," Scarlett murmured. "Yes. Let's see what kind of damage we did."

Chapter 63: The Viability Scan

Arthur gripped Scarlett's hand, the feel of her returned pressure a profound, dizzying relief. "The bassline," he repeated, his voice thick with emotion. "We won, Scarlett. It's over. Gary is gone."

She managed a fragile smile, the sheer effort evident in the tightness around her eyes. "What... what happened?" she whispered, her voice dry and unused.

"You took a bullet," Arthur explained, keeping his voice steady and clinical to avoid alarming her. "A stray round caught you in the flank. You've been resting for three weeks. Medically induced coma, to manage the systemic shock." He carefully relayed the good news. "The network is dismantled. Drayton is talking. Your intelligence won the war. Deedee and her unit are handling the clean-up."

A shadow fell across the room as the trauma doctor entered, a woman in specialized scrubs, her expression professionally cautious. "Welcome back,

Ms. Harper," the doctor said softly, approaching the bedside. "Your recovery is crucial now. We need to run some immediate checks—neurological and systemic."

The doctor efficiently checked the vitals and spoke with the nurses, ensuring Scarlett was lucid and stable after the withdrawal of sedation. The assessment was rigorous, lasting nearly ten minutes, leaving Scarlett exhausted but functional.

Once the doctor was satisfied, she dismissed the nurses and addressed Scarlett with extreme gentleness. "Ms. Harper, during the trauma stabilization, we ran a full panel of tests. Because of the nature of your injury and the chemicals found in your system, we need to bring in a specialist for further monitoring."

Scarlett frowned, confused by the medical detour. "Monitoring for what?"

The doctor gently squeezed her hand, offering a look of deep compassion. "I'll let Arthur explain the details, but we need to prioritize a very specific viability test immediately. We will return shortly." The doctor then left, giving them privacy.

The Impossible Truth

Arthur took a deep breath, knowing this was the hardest operational briefing he would ever give. He walked back to the bedside, resting his weight against the mattress, his gaze seeking hers.

"Scarlett, the specialist they mentioned... it's because of the test results," Arthur said, his voice low and firm, bracing himself for her reaction. "When they stabilized you, they found you're pregnant. You're about seven to eight weeks along now."

He felt the immediate need to provide the context that was both the source of their joy and their terror. "It happened just before the raids. It's early, and because of the physical trauma, the surgical intervention, and the residual chemical exposure... it's classified as extremely high-risk."

Scarlett stared at him, the pale features of her face shifting through disbelief, horror, and sudden, piercing understanding. The memory of their raw, urgent passion... it all clicked into horrifying, beautiful place. "No, Arthur. I can't. Not now. Not like this. Not after everything. What if it's damaged? What if it's not viable?"

Arthur pulled her hand gently to his lips, his rough skin brushing her knuckles. "I know this is impossible. This is your body, your life, and your choice. Whatever you decide, I promise you, I will stand by it. I will support your decision completely, no matter how difficult." He looked her straight in the eye, his deep brown gaze unwavering. "If you decide to keep the child, I will dedicate every second of my life to being the father it needs. This is your control, Scarlett. Your terms. Not mine."

The Viability Scan and The Job Offer

The sincerity of his promise seemed to calm the frantic terror in her mind. "A scan," Scarlett murmured. "Yes. Let's see what kind of damage we did."

The scan confirmed the small, insistent heartbeat. Arthur helped her transfer gently into a wheelchair. "Deedee is waiting right outside," he confirmed. "She has the job offer."

Deedee, dressed in civilian clothes, entered the room alone, looking exhausted but relieved. "Arthur, Scarlett," Deedee began, her voice professional but soft. "The inquiry is concluding. You're officially cleared. Headquarters wants to offer you a position: Legal Analyst, specializing in OCG financial structures. Highly paid. Completely secure."

Scarlett didn't hesitate. "I am joining the unit," she affirmed, looking at Arthur.

Just as Arthur wheeled her toward the door, a heavy voice boomed from the hallway. A large, impeccably dressed man, flanked by a rigid young aide, strode into view. Arthur stopped instantly, his hand tightening on the wheelchair grip, recognizing a new, civilian threat.

"I have secured an Ex-Parte Order of Access, Detective Jacobs!" the man, Mr. Harper, announced, his voice booming with authority. "I am invoking my familial rights to ascertain my daughter's welfare, and to secure her defense counsel!"

"I am securing your future, Scarlett!" Mr. Harper insisted, his face hardening as he saw the wheelchair. "You are now facing serious criminal charges! You need a defense strategy! I am your defense!"

Scarlett delivered the crushing blow. "I will not accept your defense."

"You will accept nothing!" Mr. Harper bellowed. "You are not thinking clearly! You will not throw away your career for this—this criminal!"

"I have already accepted a position," Scarlett affirmed, her voice steel. "Counterintelligence Counsel, Deedee. We need to start building our defense, and we start with securing full legal protection for this operation and everyone involved."

Arthur wheeled her rapidly past her father and the stunned aide. "Fan-fucking-tastic," Scarlett spat, leaning back against the wheelchair. "Nothing screams healthy pregnancy like childhood trauma and daddy issues."

"I told you," Arthur murmured, pushing her smoothly toward the elevator. "All of us. Always."

Chapter 64: The New Normal

The scent of woodsmoke and freshly brewed coffee was the new reality. It was a stark, intentional contrast to the brine and chemicals of the dockyard. Arthur stood by the window of the small, rented cottage in the remote county, watching the soft late-winter morning light fall over Scarlett. She was four months pregnant now, the visible bump a constant, profound symbol of the future they were desperately fighting to secure.

The recovery had been grueling. Scarlett's side had healed, leaving a tight, pale scar, but the trauma—both physical and psychological—was a silent tenant in the cottage. Yet, her determination had only deepened.

Arthur was officially Detective Arthur Jacobs, on specialized desk duty—a plausible cover story for his new, critical role running low-profile intelligence gathering and acting as Scarlett's exclusive, full-time protection detail from their remote sanctuary. His primary function was running constant threat assessment from the cottage; he was, inevitably, an overprotective nightmare.

The New Operational Conflict

"You're not taking the meeting downtown," he stated, his voice firm, immediately signaling the morning's conflict. He turned, leaning against the rough stone of the windowsill.

Scarlett was already dressed—not in her old solicitor's silk, but in comfortable, practical clothing—reviewing encrypted files on her government-issued secure laptop. "I am Counterintelligence Counsel; I need to assess the veracity of the evidence directly. I need to be in the room to gauge the reactions of the financial investigators. I'm not sitting here running property filings all day. I have a job to do."

"You have a high-risk job," he corrected, stepping closer. "Our enemy is still out there. Gary is wounded, not dead. We know he's consolidating. He knows you are the structural weak point in my defense—the fastest way to break me is to threaten you. You take the meeting via secure video link. I go in, wearing a wire, with a full Met security detail."

Scarlett closed the laptop with a decisive click, meeting his gaze. "The frozen accounts are being drained through new front companies in Eastern Europe," she reported, shifting the conversation to the substance of the threat. "We are hunting a ghost who is two steps ahead. I need autonomy to execute the next phase of the investigation."

The tension in the cottage was immense—a battle between Arthur's tactical imperative to secure his family and Scarlett's professional need to leverage her unique legal insight.

The Last Command

"Jade's meeting with Deedee this afternoon," Arthur reminded her, keeping his voice carefully level. Jade, having survived the immediate fallout of the raid, was now cooperating fully, providing an invaluable civilian perspective on Gary's local operations. "Until then, you stay in this house. That's an order, lawyer."

Scarlett recognized the finality in his tone. She didn't argue further. She pushed herself up from the desk, carrying the heavy weight of her frustration, and walked slowly to the small, empty spare room—their planned nursery. The room was currently bare, waiting for a future they had not yet earned. She placed her hand over her abdomen, feeling a tiny, insistent flutter—the life demanding security, consistency, and survival.

"Fine. I'll run the meeting from the secure link," she conceded, turning back. "But if I'm staying here, I need coffee, and I need to know you're wearing your new trauma plate."

Arthur understood. She was demanding proof that he valued his life as much as he valued hers. He patted his chest, confirming the presence of the lightweight, bullet-resistant vest he wore under his civilian clothes.

He pulled her into a fierce embrace, his good arm wrapping gently but firmly around the small bump, the gesture a silent promise to the life within. He rested his chin against the top of her head, inhaling the woodsmoke and coffee scent that defined their borrowed safety.

"I love you, Arthur," she murmured.

"I know," he replied. "Now, let's go hunt a ghost."

Chapter 65: The Arsenal of Domesticity

The illusion of peace was fragile, brittle, and maintained only by constant vigilance. The cottage was clean, the wood-burning stove was lit, and Scarlett was safe, working on the old wooden desk that served as their operations center, but Arthur saw the danger in everything. The high windows were vulnerabilities. The stove was a heat signature. Their new routine was an elaborate, necessary lie.

Their mornings were dominated by training. Arthur taught Scarlett weapon retention and low-impact evasion—exploiting an attacker's balance, using distraction, and leveraging her environment. He demanded continuous drills to sharpen her reflexes. "Again," Arthur instructed, watching Scarlett practice drawing the unloaded sidearm from its hidden position beneath the couch cushions. "Faster, Scarlett. If they breach, you don't hesitate. You fire to disable, then you fucking run." The training felt absurd against the backdrop of the baby catalogs she now kept hidden under her laptop, catalogs filled with tiny wool booties and soft, unnecessary toys. She had painted the tiny spare room a soft, neutral grey—a clean slate for a life that deserved purity, not paranoia.

The Radek Revelation

"Did you find the primary accountant for the Aethelred Group?" Arthur asked, interrupting her drill with operational necessity.

"I found the accountant, Arthur. And I found the perfect mobile for the crib," she replied, executing a precise sweep of her periphery before setting the pistol down. "The accountant is a Mr. Radek in Prague. He handles multiple offshore trusts. He's the key to tracing Gary's liquid funds." She leaned back. "And yes, you massive git, I finished my drill. Now put the bloody gun away."

The discovery of Mr. Radek—a central figure in Gary's money laundering scheme—gave them a new, concrete target. The focus of their work shifted from defense to offense.

Code Red vs. Morning Sickness

Their first major argument erupted that evening while they were making dinner, the friction of their two irreconcilable realities finally igniting.

"You left the security protocol log open!" Arthur snapped, his voice tight with controlled fury as he pointed at the screen. "What the hell were you thinking? That log tracks the drone sweep and the frequency jammers! It's the most valuable piece of counter-intel we have!"

"I was checking the Land Registry filings for properties under Radek's name, Arthur!" Scarlett shouted back, tears of pain and frustration immediately springing to her eyes. "I had to run to the loo because I was pumping my bloody gut up for ten minutes straight! I couldn't bloody save the session!"

Arthur's posture instantly dissolved, the police operative replaced by the terrified partner. He moved toward her, his movements swift. "Jesus, are you alright? Is it pain? Is it the wound?"

"It's the baby, Arthur! It's morning sickness! It's six weeks of nausea! I cannot live in a constant state of Code Red when I'm barely keeping crackers down! You need to trust ME to handle the house while you handle the outside!" she cried, the need for normalcy overriding tactical sense.

"I only trust what I can see and what I can break, Scarlett!" he countered, his voice raw with the depth of his anxiety. "You are the highest value target I have ever protected, and you are carrying my child! My professional training demands total control over your environment! You are going to lose both of us if you don't let down the armor sometimes. Let us be normal!"

The Truce

A moment of heavy, shared silence followed, defined by the steam rising from the stove and the sound of the wind. Scarlett looked at the fear etched on his face, understanding that his vigilance was love.

"Fine," she conceded, the anger draining away, leaving her exhausted. "I think Jonesy would take one look at your security setup and demand triple hazard pay." She smiled faintly, referencing the fact that their cat was now safely lodged with Deedee.

Arthur pulled her close, his embrace fierce but careful around her waist. "I am sorry. I will reset the parameters." He knew he was asking the impossible: to trust an environment he couldn't control. "Let's just focus on getting Mr. Radek. He's our weak point."

He lowered his head, pressing his lips to her forehead. "Normalcy is our greatest weakness, Scarlett. But it's also our only reason to fight."

Chapter 66: The Logan Protocol

The hospital basement room was silent, clean, and dominated by the high-resolution monitor. Arthur sat beside Scarlett, his hand clamped over her own, his face a blend of profound concentration and deep-seated terror, watching the medical team prepare the screen. Jonesy, their ginger tabby, now lived with them in the cottage, a persistent, furry shadow who acted as their silent, demanding housemate.

The sonographer cleared her throat. "Do you both want to know the gender today, or keep it a surprise?"

"Yes, absolutely," Scarlett said instantly, leaning forward, the solicitor in her demanding actionable data.

"No," Arthur countered, his voice flat.

Scarlett whipped her head toward him, already hormonal and irritable. "Arthur! We're spending our entire cash reserve on baby supplies! I need to know if I'm buying bloody pink dresses or miniature combat trousers. Stop being dramatic! The mission is the baby, you complete bellend! And the mission requires adequate storage solutions! Boy or girl? We need to know!"

The sonographer announced brightly, "Congratulations. You're having a boy."

The word—*boy*—hit Arthur with the force of a high-velocity round. He saw the future—a vulnerable life he was absolutely bound to protect. "A boy," he repeated, the sound rough with sudden, final acceptance. "We'll call him Logan."

Scarlett squeezed his hand, her own eyes bright with tears. "Logan. I love it."

Arthur leaned his head against her shoulder. "I don't know how to do this," he whispered, the admission raw. "I grew up in the system, Scarlett. I don't know how to build a safe home. I only know how to dismantle threats."

"Oh, for fuck's sake, Arthur," she sighed, her tone gentle but firm. "We are starting from ground zero. We learn as we go. We are going to be chaotic, brilliant, and utterly unprepared, just like we are now. And we will be the safest family on the planet because we are the only two people who know where to hide the bodies."

The Domestic Siege

Their life settled into a strained new domestic routine defined by total seclusion. Arthur managed all external logistics: all necessary baby supplies were bought online and delivered to a network of decoy houses used by Deedee's unit, ensuring the cottage address remained completely dark. Scarlett only left the cottage when Arthur personally escorted her to the secure Manchester Met office for necessary briefings, their cover story being that she was working remotely as a legal consultant.

Meanwhile, Mr. Harper, Scarlett's father, was a relentless, powerful liability. His legal team, convinced she was being held against her will by a "criminal" (Arthur), kept sending costly litigation and Ex-Parte Orders to Deedee's unit base demanding welfare checks and access. Each order was squashed by Scarlett, who, as Counterintelligence Counsel, legally dismissed her father's intrusive filings, but the pressure was constant.

The vigil continued nightly. Arthur often watched her sleep, his fears manifesting as quiet protection.

> *He held a strong, steady hand over her growing bump, talking in a low, conspiratorial murmur he assumed she couldn't hear. "They're hunting us, Logan. But she's building a home for us anyway. We protect the home, you hear me? We protect your mum."*

The Bomb and the Secret

Scarlett was, in fact, fully aware of his nightly vigil. She enjoyed the private, raw tenderness. However, her pregnancy, now visibly advanced, was turning her into a deeply hormonal, unpredictable force. She went from professional focus to sudden, tearful rage within minutes. "The personality of a bomb," Arthur had once muttered, only half-joking.

The reality of the Logan Protocol—total isolation and anonymous online purchasing—was creating a critical domestic bottleneck.

(Time Jump: 6 Months Pregnant / 24 Weeks)

Scarlett stared at the generic, military-spec baby items Arthur had meticulously vetted and secured via decoy drops. The basic white baby monitor and the industrial-gray car seat were safe, but utterly soulless.

"Arthur," she stated, her voice tight with uncharacteristic frustration. "This is Logan. Not a hostage. This car seat looks like it's designed for riot control. I'm building a nursery, not a bunker."

The need for designer, comfortable, specific baby gear—the high-grade car seat, the non-hackable monitoring system, the specific fabrics—was growing critical. She needed items that couldn't be sourced without specialized retail access. Deedee's team couldn't source these items without drawing massive attention.

Over the next week, a subtle, secretive plan began to form in Scarlett's mind. If the unit couldn't source the goods, and Arthur wouldn't risk leaving the cottage, she would have to violate the primary rule herself. Her high-value, civilian profile was the only way to get the items without raising an alert within the Met. The cottage was stifling. She was going to London.

The confrontation with Arthur would have to wait. The planning for her final act of reckless love—a solo supply run for Logan—was now underway.

Chapter 67: The Aethelred Trap

The low-burning fire cast dancing shadows across the rough stone walls of the cottage, illuminating the map spread across the wooden table. The pressure from Mr. Harper was relentless, and the need to end the OCG threat was absolute.

Arthur was meticulously cleaning the stolen sidearm, his good arm moving with quiet, focused efficiency. Scarlett was leaning over the map, her attention locked on a network of highlighted properties and subsidiary names she had uncovered since their last run. She was focused on the biggest, most resilient shell company: the Aethelred Group.

"This is not negotiable, Arthur. I am the Counterintelligence Counsel," Scarlett stated, her voice sharp with professional clarity. "I need eyes on the physical location of the asset transfer that Radek is coordinating. Freezing the accounts is Phase One; Phase Two is catching the transfer of the assets themselves."

Arthur stopped cleaning the weapon, his gaze hardening. "You are the high-value target. I am the unseen variable. I go."

"You are pregnant! Six months! I am not putting the child at risk for a quarter-million pounds of illicit funds, even if it is critical evidence!"

Scarlett stood up, placing her hands on the table, her body language challenging his order. "You are the known target, Arthur. Your face, your methods, your tactical profile—it's all compromised. I am the unseen variable. I am a pregnant woman, a civilian lawyer. They are looking for a broken soldier, not a woman doing a welfare check."

Arthur finally sagged, running a hand over his tired face. "Fine. We compromise. We don't go to the transfer. We go to the asset's location. The properties themselves. We both go to London, but we move by train, not car—it's less traceable against ANPR, and we blend better. We observe only."

Phase I: Preparing the Asset

The days leading up to the trip were consumed by rigorous, covert preparation. Arthur had accepted the inevitability of the risk but demanded total control over the operational parameters.

He spent hours teaching Scarlett weapons handling—not live fire, but muscle memory and safety protocols. He demonstrated how to check the chamber, how to hold the weapon steady, and, most importantly, weapon retention—how to keep the pistol out of the hands of the enemy.

"Your physical defense training focuses on low-impact neutralization and evasion," he instructed, watching her practice small, precise shifts of weight. "Your job is not to fight; it is to buy time for my backup." He repeated the mantra until it was ingrained: "Your job is not to fight; it is to buy time."

Meanwhile, the pressure from her father continued. Mr. Harper's legal assault on Deedee's unit was persistent and aggressive, costing the Met thousands in legal hours. Scarlett quietly and efficiently signed the paperwork to legally dismiss her father's firm as her counsel, officially ceding her defense to the Met's internal legal team and severing her father's last legal link to her.

Phase II: The London Infiltration

"We take the train into London early tomorrow morning," Arthur finalized, folding the map, his voice gaining its tactical precision. "We use different forms of transport from the station, losing ourselves in the city crowd. You look capable, you look busy. You are the last thing a security team expects to see—a pregnant woman on a business trip. I, meanwhile, will be your shadow."

Scarlett felt the familiar spike of adrenaline and anticipation. The plan was audacious, relying entirely on the chaos of the city and the sheer absurdity of their profiles.

"The Aethelred Group is the centerpiece of the whole operation," Scarlett affirmed, tracing the names on the paper. "If we hit that transfer, we provide the final piece of irrefutable evidence Deedee needs to completely dismantle the network and secure our defense."

The success of the entire operation rested entirely on Scarlett's ability to remain calm and Arthur's ability to stay true to his promise: he was her shield, and she was the weapon. The train tickets were bought, the tactical bag packed, and the countdown to the final, high-stakes surveillance mission was underway.

Here is the full, logically corrected Chapter 68, detailing the emotional proposal and the high-stakes planning for the final supply run to London.

Chapter 68: The Bothy Proposal

Scarlett was now seven and a half months pregnant. She was fundamentally clumsy, perpetually off-balance, and her body was a source of constant, minor rebellion. Getting out of the low armchair felt like a specialized combat maneuver—a slow, grunting heave followed by deep, necessary breathing. Arthur watched her like a highly valuable, slightly unstable explosive device. His surveillance was now purely domestic, but no less intense.

"Arthur, I am three seconds away from peeing myself," she retorted, exasperated by his rigid attention as she tried to navigate the small room. "And I can assure you, the state of my bladder is not a tactical vulnerability."

He responded instantly, pushing off the stone wall where he habitually stood guard. "The vulnerability is the time-on-target exposure if you have to run unexpectedly," he countered, though his eyes held amusement.

"We traced the Aethelred Group funds to three separate European accounts," Arthur reported, shifting the conversation back to the work, his voice professional. "He's financing his last stand—a network of high-value decoys—but he's running on fumes. He's liquidating."

The tactical data didn't mitigate the domestic crisis. "Did you seriously forget to order the bloody garlic bread again?" she shrieked, the volume shocking. "You had one simple job, you incompetent prick!"

Arthur, pushed past his breaking point by the relentless surveillance and fear, snapped back, his voice low and tight with frustrated rage. "Well, I better go get some fucking garlic bread then!"

The rage snapped instantly into despair. "No, don't go!" she suddenly wailed, the anger dissolving into violent, hyperventilating sobs as Arthur cautiously backed away from the sudden emotional blast radius. "He's so cute, Arthur! And Jonesy! Oh my god, he's so cute, I'm going to miss him so much!"

The sight of her collapse—her face contorted with genuine, profound pain—killed his anger instantly. "Oh, Jesus, Scarlett. I'm sorry," Arthur whispered, moving toward her.

Arthur gently scooped her up, tucking her against his uninjured side, understanding the volatility was a product of fear and hormones, not actual rage.

The Proposal

Later that evening, after the crying spell subsided, they were curled up on the sofa under the thick wool blanket.

Arthur pulled her closer, shifting her head onto his chest. He began singing—low, gentle, and utterly sincere—the melody of a song she recognized. He focused on the most poignant lyrics, his voice rough with emotion and the unspoken history they shared.

"If you needed someone, I'm the one who'd run, I'm the one who'd run to you..." he sang, the sound raw and full of the weight of his sacrifice.

He continued, his hand slowly reaching into his trouser pocket while his eyes stayed locked on hers: *"I will hold you when the water's rough, I will trust you when the world gives up, I'm the one who'd run to you..."*

He reached into his pocket and pulled out the small velvet pouch. He opened the pouch, revealing a simple silver band set with the smooth, polished, grey river stone. The stone was dull and beautiful, a world away from diamonds.

"It's from the bothy creek," he whispered, pressing the simple ring into her palm. "I don't have diamonds, Scarlett. I just have certainty."

He met her gaze, his dark eyes intense, reflecting the clean light of the fire. "Will you marry me, lawyer? We build our home right here, in the eye of the storm. I am yours."

She whispered, "Yes," tears mixing with the song's melody.

The Final Run Setup

The proposal had provided emotional clarity, but the tactical reality remained. "But Arthur, Logan needs the high-grade car seat, the secure monitor," she reminded him, urgency returning to her voice. "Deedee can't source it without red flags. We need to finalize the decoy drops for the specialist equipment."

Arthur looked at the map. "The logistics are too complex for a regional hub like Manchester for those items. We need to hit a major commercial city with centralized, anonymous suppliers. We have to go to London." He took a deep, shaky breath, the risk immediately evident. "The trip must happen when you're 37 weeks—no sooner. That's the perfect cover. No one pays attention to a heavily pregnant woman doing some last-minute baby shopping."

Scarlett shook her head, her mind instantly shifting to operational protection. "No, Arthur. You are the known target. If they get you, they get Logan and me. I go. My civilian profile is the safest bet. I will wear the wire, and I will be out in an hour."

A profound fear crossed Arthur's face. He knew she was right. Her civilian profile was their only clean asset left. The argument had shifted from *if* the risk would be taken, to *who* would take it.

"Fine," he conceded, the word tight with utter dread. "We plan it to the second. You are going to London for the supplies, and I am going to be the silent overwatch, two blocks away. This is our last run, Scarlett. The last risk before the birth."

Chapter 69: The Final Countdown

Scarlett was now thirty-seven weeks pregnant, just days from her due date. Her profile was no longer just highly visible; it was immense and awkward. She moved with the slow, careful dignity of someone carrying a secret, and that secret was Logan. Arthur was planning for the safe, traceable, and ultimately predictable Manchester regional run—the trip she had agreed to take to finalize supplies. She, however, had made her final, critical decision. The Manchester trip was the decoy. The true mission was London.

She watched Arthur pace the cottage, the floorboards groaning under his weight, detailing the safe routes into Manchester. He was worried, but convinced he had calculated every risk. His trust in her adherence to the plan—his plan—was the precise vulnerability she was counting on.

The deception had been built piece by piece over weeks. She knew Arthur relied on constant, verifiable data. She retrieved the secondary burner phone she had purchased anonymously during their last drive—a lifeline known only to her. Her next move was far more dangerous than simple communication.

She reached inside the old operations backpack, the one salvaged from the initial chaos, and pulled out the switchblade—a nasty, untraceable weapon Michael had dropped in the sub-level interrogation room. The cold steel felt shocking and strangely empowering in her hand. She secured the knife deep inside her handbag, burying it beneath a stack of newly laundered baby clothes. It wasn't a gun, but it was a close-quarters equalizer, and it was hers alone.

The Meticulous Deception

The logistics for the deception were meticulous. She had secured the train tickets two days prior, purchasing them in cash from a secluded regional station using a temporary, pre-paid debit card—a paper trail that would lead to a dead end.

Her most critical step was neutralizing Arthur's surveillance. She checked the small, hidden tracking chip Arthur had insisted she wear in the lining of her heavy maternity coat. Using the technique she had learned while hacking the Land Registry databases, she executed a complex location spoof on the chip, feeding it a pre-recorded path of travel toward Manchester. The chip would transmit a steady, plausible signal—Arthur, relying on the GPS signal, would be securing a perimeter around a ghost.

The choice of target was deliberate. She was heading straight to London—the place Arthur had deemed too hot, too visible, and too risky for either of them. She was going to hit Harrods, Hamleys, and the high-end boutiques where the specialized, unhackable monitoring gear and the high-grade car seat were sold. She would rely on the total absurdity of her profile—a hugely pregnant, injured woman shopping designer goods in cash—as her best camouflage. Who would suspect a mother-to-be of running a top-tier OCG counter-operation? The sheer audacity was the safest disguise.

The Emotional Cost

She dressed slowly, choosing comfortable but expensive-looking layers—a final, deliberate act of reclaiming her former life, now woven with threads of deep deception. The weight of the baby and the weight of the lie were almost unbearable. She felt a profound loneliness, knowing she was carrying the full operational burden of the final run, while simultaneously betraying the trust of the man who had risked his life for her.

She stood in the quiet nursery, running her hand over the soft grey paint. She was thirty-seven weeks pregnant, alone, and hunting designer baby clothes. She whispered to the life inside her, her voice trembling slightly, "You deserve better than police-issue gray, Logan. You deserve beautiful chaos. And I'm going to get it for you."

Arthur found her by the window, watching the sunrise. He gave her a final, nervous kiss, checking the zipper of her coat one last time, confirming the signal's position. He was worried, but convinced he had covered every angle.

"I'll be twenty minutes ahead of you, securing the first sector of Manchester," he promised, his voice low with tension. "Text me immediately when you board the train." He touched the coat lining, confirming the signal's position was stable.

He had no idea she had gone completely off-map. She was heading to the very heart of the capital, relying on her skills, her wits, and the knife secured deep in her handbag. The moment Arthur stepped out the door and started driving toward Manchester, the final countdown began, sending Scarlett Hurtling toward a fate neither of them could have predicted.

Chapter 70: The Bassline's Final Demand

Arthur slammed his hand down on the unit terminal. The screen displayed two small green trajectory lines. The first dot (the spoofed coat tracker) was moving steadily towards Manchester. The second dot, labeled *CONVERSE*, was moving fast—into the heart of the capital. She didn't use the secure protocol. She went rogue. She went shopping.

The betrayal was swift and absolute, yet quickly transmuted into cold, professional fury. He knew instantly she had taken the risk he had forbidden, but his own protective measure—the second, secret tracker he'd stitched into her favorite battered Converse—was the only reason he knew where she really was.

Arthur started barking orders to the unit team—a mix of Deedee's clean officers and contracted IT analysts. "Bypass the GPS filter, for Christ's sake! Check the central city traffic feeds now! I need eyes on the Knightsbridge perimeter!"

The screens—fed by city CCTV and covert Met feeds—switched instantly to a montage of real-time traffic feeds across London's Knightsbridge district. Arthur watched, a frantic, impotent observer, his heart hammering a painful rhythm against his ribs.

The Reckless Shopping Spree

Arthur watched the nightmare unfold in high definition. Scarlett had transformed herself from a determined operative into a conspicuous, wealthy tourist.

He saw her exit a high-end buggy shop, pausing at the curb to speak with a concierge. On screen, Scarlett paid cash, accepting a small, sleek electronic box and a receipt. "She's collecting the monitoring system," Arthur muttered, translating the action. "She arranged the delivery of the buggy itself to one of Deedee's dead drop addresses. A fucking latte, Scarlett, really?"

He watched her walk to an adjacent boutique, bags—mostly small, patterned carrier bags—swinging from her arm. She paused, checked her reflection in the window, and actually smiled.

The chaos of her consumption was maddeningly effective camouflage. No one looked twice at a heavily pregnant woman laden with expensive bags. But every second she stayed on the street, the risk multiplied.

The Fatal Error

After what felt like an eternity, Scarlett appeared to have finished her spree. She moved away from the main commercial street, heading toward the nearest Underground station.

Arthur saw it on the CCTV feed: the dark, unmarked Mercedes Vito van pulled sharply into the side street, cutting off her path to the Underground. Arthur recognized the vehicle. Gary stepped out of the driver's door.

Scarlett was trapped on the pavement. The mercenary, flanked by two other men—all massive and wearing dark, non-uniform jackets—advanced rapidly. Gary remained near the van, watching.

Arthur watched, his vision blurring. He saw the capture happening on the screen, but the clarity of the *how* was a terrifying deduction. Gary hadn't tracked the devices; he had tracked the narrative.

The three men immediately surrounded Scarlett. She reacted instantly, dropping her bags, trying to swing her bulky body and retrieve the switchblade. The limitations of her pregnancy were brutally clear.

A passerby—a young man with headphones—saw the immediate violence and hesitated. He tried to intervene, shouting and rushing the attackers. Arthur screamed silently at the screen, knowing the folly. One of the flanking mercenaries pulled a suppressed pistol and shot the passerby in the head with brutal efficiency. The young man dropped instantly.

Scarlett went instantly rigid, her brief moment of resistance broken by the sudden, lethal violence, her hands flew to her abdomen in pure, protective surrender. The men didn't have to drag her. They simply escorted her, her immense body an awkward burden, into the back of the van.

The GPS signal—the small, tenacious green dot that represented Scarlett's life, the only reliable link they had—went DARK as the tracking wire in her coat was inevitably severed inside the van. Arthur roared, his voice tearing as he slammed his fist onto the console. "Goddammit!"

"Forget the coat chip, follow the Converse signal!" Arthur screamed, realizing the primary tracking method was still active. "The Converse is our only lock! Track the last known location of the *Converse* signal, you incompetent bastards!"

The screens switched instantly to a montage of general London traffic feeds, uselessly trying to locate a single black van among millions of vehicles. Arthur watched the vehicle drive away, his anger giving way to cold, paralyzing despair.

Then, the terrible realization hit him. He saw Gary's face—the ultimate triumph—in his mind. "That smug bastard," Arthur whispered, his voice broken, his throat raw. "He didn't need the electronics. He just ran her mugshot on the city feeds. He used the 'Bonnie and Clyde' news story as a manhunt weapon."

He stood up, shoving the chair aside. "Firebreak protocol," Arthur dictated, his voice now flat, operational, and lethal. "Full tactical deployment. I'm going to London. Get me a transport vehicle with a clean route. I need all available local feeds routed to my screen. We bring her home, and we end the bassline for good."